Mike,
Here's to your
pursuit of Le
all the best,

Jim Heinken
'18

IN PURSUIT OF LOVE

JIM HAMILTON

LIBRARY TALES PUBLISHING

Published by:
Library Tales Publishing, Inc.
www.LibraryTalesPublishing.com
www.Facebook.com/LibraryTalesPublishing

Copyright © 2014 by James F. Hamilton

No part of this publication may be reproduced, stored in a retrieval system, or transmitted in any form or by any means, electronic, mechanical, photocopying, recording, scanning, or otherwise, except as permitted under Sections 107 or 108 of the 1976 United States Copyright Act, without the prior written permission of the Publisher.

Trademarks: Library Tales Publishing, Library Tales, the Library Tales Publishing logo, and related trade dress are trademarks or registered trademarks of Library Tales Publishing, Inc. and/or its affiliates in the United States and other countries, and may not be used without written permission. All other trademarks are the property of their respective owners.

For general information on our other products and services, please contact our Customer Care Department at 1-800-754-5016, or fax 917-463-0892. For technical support, please e-mail Office@Librarytales.com

Library Tales Publishing also publishes its books in a variety of electronic formats. Every content that appears in print is available in electronic books.

ISBN-13: 978-0615970813
ISBN-10: 0615970818

PRINTED IN THE UNITED STATES OF AMERICA

Praise for
IN PURSUIT OF LOVE

"***In Pursuit of Love*** was a thought provoking journey through the life of a well-intentioned man, who accidentally allowed work to get in the way of his relationships. I appreciated learning from his mistakes, and found myself grateful for the journey."

— John Naber, Olympic Champion, Sports Announcer, Motivational Speaker and Author

* * *

"Jim Hamilton's ***In Pursuit of Love*** is not half full but instead brimming with genies and wisdom for about every executive in the fast lane of life. This *"can't put me down"* read moves quickly to the heart of the distractions that keep us from what matters most. You will love this book that will serve as an early detection sign for life's most important lesson."

—Jeffrey Patnaude, author of *Leading from the Maze, Living Simultaneously, Habits of Heroes and Wisdom of the Father.*

* * *

"Jim Hamilton provides readers with a wonderfully quick and introspective view of life's priorities through the very honest and relatable main character Tom Daniels. The enjoyable read allows for vicarious self-reflection."

—Jennifer Stanford, CEO, Emergent Performance Solutions

"It's been said that wisdom is experience well digested. Hiding in plain sight is the obviously well digested experience and wisdom that Jim Hamilton brings to his semi-autobiographical parable *In Pursuit of Love.* In it, the reader finds a reckoning and accounting of what is worth striving for and a reminder that it can too easily slip away. The style is fresh, immediate and direct. One can imagine being in the presence of the author, hearing his story in person over a cup of coffee and not being able to resist thinking about and responding with your own resonant tale. Lacking that opportunity, we can be thankful that Mr. Hamilton has had the courage to look frankly into the mirror and share his reflections in this well told tale."

—Bob Kanegis, Ambassador to The Realm of Possibilities at Tales & Trails Storytelling

* * *

"Was it just a coincidence this hit a little too close to home? As a professional 'suit,' struggling in an ongoing pursuit for 'more', juggling a loving wife and children, I paused to reflect after reading Jim Hamilton's *In Pursuit of Love*. Ingeniously borrowing Dickens' what-if literary device, the (familiar to us all) protagonist is shown what his life could be if he continued on his current path. This was a gut-wrenching reminder of not only my life – but of countless people in all walks of life. The pursuit of 'more' versus the appreciation of the love we may already have all around us. Where's Love is a beautiful allegory, woven with quality writing and cast with well-written, fully-developed characters that will be familiar in all readers' lives. It's okay if this tale hits close to home – and that's why you should read it."

—Richard Wickliffe, Author of *Memories of Holly Woode* and in leadership in a Fortune 50 Corporation

IT'S ALL ABOUT HER
By Jim Hamilton

Paperback: 146 pages
Language: English
ISBN: 978-0615748009
List Price: $16.99
www.ItsAllAboutHer.Net

The multitude of pressures that lead relationships between couples from their starting point of love, passion, respect, and hope to apathy, complacency, repetitiveness, and discouragement are often allowed to take hold, rendering the outlook for many relationships bleak. Women spend millions to find solutions in books and therapy. The hunt is for the approach that will solve their marital problems -- or at least "fix" their spouse. Written by a man and for men, It's All About Her speaks to everyday problem-solving and relationship-improving in practical, playful, and more than occasionally profound ways. Is it the last word on interpersonal relationships? No. A new interpretation of the planetary origins of the male and female psyches? Absolutely not. A simple, easy-to-read set of suggestions that any guy can try to enhance the fun, respect, excitement, and love in his marriage? Yes! Delivered in a straightforward, witty, and thought-provoking style, **It's Al About Her** is designed to spur actions and insights that work in the real world. It provide dozens of how-to's for everything from giving gifts and sharing a bathroom to entertaining, teaming on the career front, and even attending the kids' sporting events. Some are about fun, some romance, some respect but all enhance the relationship – and recall the basics that often fall by the wayside in long-term, side-by-side living.

Jim Hamilton is a 50-something business consultant with over 30 years of experience in the hi-tech industry. More importantly, he is a father of three, grandfather of three, and husband to one remarkable woman. Author of *It's All About Her: A Man-to-Man's Guide to Marital Bliss*, he is recognized for his insightful, entertaining, and humorous writing style. Through his writing, national interviews, and blogging, he is on a mission to help couples improve their relationships by enhancing the way they communicate, connect, and care for one another. "Good is not good enough," he says. "We should all strive toward a happier and more fulfilling life through having a phenomenal marriage."

A graduate of UCLA, Jim was brought up in Palo Alto, CA, and currently resides in Pleasanton, CA with his extraordinary his wife, Dora.

TABLE OF CONTENTS

Chapter I	Presence of Mind	3
Chapter II	Memory Lane	15
Chapter III	Present Tense	56
Chapter IV	Possibilities	77
Chapter V	The New Norm	112
Chapter VI	His World	128
Chapter VII	My Breadcrumbs	129

Dedicated to all those asking "Why me?"
with my encouragement to move to "What now?"
The power is within and about you.

CHAPTER I
PRESENCE OF MIND

The sharp pain that shot through his leg yanked him to attention or at least to as much consciousness as the knot on his head would allow. Similar to the disorientation experienced when one receives that errant phone call in a hotel room in the middle of the night, he wasn't all there mentally.

"Ouch! Damn!" he mumbled, as he tried to move. The reports were coming in from his extremities, serving notice that all of his body parts were there, even if they were not in very good shape.

Clearly he wasn't in the backyard of his upscale suburban home outside of Silicon Valley in Northern

California.

"What the hell? Shit!" The stabbing feeling in his knee helped to accelerate his awareness of his current environment...an awareness that he was beginning to regret. A steady rain was falling on him and he was saturated. It wasn't the torrential downpour associated with the thunderstorms in other parts of the country. It was the steady light rain that was common in Northern California between November and April.

As he slowly opened his eyes, he was starting to believe that he was in deep trouble.

He grappled with how to improve his current situation, but the only progress he seemed to be able to make was a little clarity as to how he had arrived at his current location. The details slowly revealed themselves. Adding to his confused state, or maybe because of it, his recollection of the events preceding his awakening came back to him in reverse order. It was as though he had hit the slow rewind on his DVR at home. Home, that's where he was headed.

Plunging down the side of the hill.

Sharp turn to the right.

Loss of control.

On-coming lights appearing out of nowhere.

The monotonous slapping of the wiper blades.

The road.

He knew where he was, but at the same time felt lost. He was heading home, taking the route he had travelled so many times that his BMW 7-series knew the way. He really didn't need to drive, just needed to keep his foot on the pedal, catch every word from the sports talk radio show on KNBR, and be prepared to answer any call that would come through on his cell phone.

His car. Where the hell was his car? He attempted to turn around to look for it only to be reminded of what must be a pretty significant injury to his knee and an increasingly painful throbbing in his head. What he could finally conclude was that it was dark, very dark, and quiet, save for the intermittent sound of cars above him in the distance.

As his eyes adjusted to the lighting, he saw what he believed to be the outline of his car below him. The failure of his seatbelt to keep him in his car as it had careened down the hill, while inexplicable, may have saved his life, given the destruction to his car he could see. The car and the cloud of smoke emanating from the front end of it, appeared to be about 50 yards farther down the hill, but in the shape he was in it might just as well have been 50 miles away. His spot assessment was that he was not going to reach it anytime soon.

The series of events that brought him to his current state again rushed into his mind, but this time the DVR was functioning better and moving forward. He had been on his way home from work, late as usual, after another 12-hour day. Whether it was the early spring storm; the dark road, made more so by the cloud cover; his fatigue and the late hour; or the asshole behind those oncoming lights, he was still not able to fully deduce the cause of the accident that led to his current predicament. What he did know was that he was apparently stuck on a ledge on the side of a hill. He was soaked, but strangely did not feel any sensation of temperature.

"Gotta get help," he thought. "My Cell!"

He just needed to call his wife or 911 and someone

could get out here to help him. He could hear the traffic above and had a general idea of where he was. The "country"part of his commute was only about 10 miles long. They would find him.

"Whew," he said aloud, feeling a sense of relief. He instinctively reached for his cell phone on the car console to his right.

"Godammit," signaled his reversal of emotions as he remembered he was no longer in his car, he had no idea where the cell phone was, and that he possessed a limited ability to search for it. He briefly reflected on how he might want to reconsider his vanity-based decision to never wear a phone clip on his belt. But he quickly regained his version of sensibility, concluding that the current inconvenience of not having his cell phone handy was just the price for avoiding being tagged with the "geek" label.

A brief moment of clarity and a huge shot of pain in his head brought him to two new conclusions: He was a snobbish, shallow asshole, and he may very well be in some serious trouble. He could live with the first, as he had for the better part of his 44 years, but the second was a bit more problematic.

Whether it was the shock that his body had experienced wearing off or his newfound awareness of just how bad his situation was, he started to feel cold. Wet and cold. Wet, cold, and hurting. A sense of urgency bordering on panic, to do something, anything, came over him. As his eyes further adjusted to the dark night, he could now see a few yards away that there was a small indent to the hill next to a very large tree. He concluded that at the very least, if he could just get over to that "cave" he would be able to get out of the rain, a rain which had progressed from a drizzle to a pretty steady downpour.

A turn to his right, a knife in the knee, a club to the head. For some reason it kept surprising him. He was reminded of one of his favorite (and too often used) sayings: The definition of insanity is repeating the same thing and expecting different results. But it was clear that the pain was unavoidable and he better just suck it up.

He needed to get some shelter. Shelter from the Storm. He hadn't thought of that Dylan song for years.

"Stop it!" he thought. He needed to focus. Every problem had a solution…a fix. He just needed to keep his wits about him and he would solve this one. "Stay focused!"

Pulling himself over the leafy mat that covered the muddy slope, he dragged his left leg and pushed with his right. "Damn," he thought. "I'm going to have to get that scoped again," remembering the two previous procedures he had endured. It was the price he had paid for being the weekend warrior on the soccer field, without having spent the time to stay in soccer shape or good general condition, for that matter. He finally traversed what seemed to be a mile to his "cave", his Man Cave. "I finally have my Man Cave! Look what you had to go through to get it," he said to himself.

Strangely his thoughts now shot to the numerous, not-so-positive discussions he had with his wife about his need for "space", both physically and emotionally. "Be careful what you ask for," he thought.

As he adjusted his body to a position that was as comfortable as he could get, he started thinking of options and concluded that he really had none until it got much later and his wife realized he was late, very late, even for him. Without the ability to move any great distance and the absence of any communication device, he was pretty well stuck for a while.

Given his recent track record, "late" had a new meaning. His wife, his lovely wife, Denise. His thoughts were mixed by the firm belief that he really did love her and thought that she was lovely, but that lately, things just weren't right. He chuckled, "Lately." How long was "lately"? What had happened? When did it happen? Why did it happen? "Forget it," he thought, "things are fine, I'm just feeling sorry for myself because of the accident and I'm hurt. Someone will find me."

How long would that take?

Another shiver went through his body. He had always been a glass half-full kind of guy, although tonight seemed to have the potential to change that. He wasn't sure if it was cold or the fear generated by the possibility that he might not be missed for many hours. Late had become the new early, so much so that his wife had even given up the periodic questioning of whether he was really at work all those late evenings. He now concluded that there was one positive aspect of having let himself go physically over the last 10 years: no woman in her right mind, with a shred of taste, would consider him a candidate for an affair or a sexual liaison, unless he wanted to pay for it, which he didn't and never had.

He remembered that awkward questioning from his wife. All the circumstantial evidence was there: the late hours and regular out-of-town travel; the increasing number of women in the hi-tech industry; and the ascension of many women to senior executive positions within his company who were acting as role models for numerous young, highly educated and capable new female entrants into the game. He wasn't threatened by this, as they needed what industry veterans like him had: industry knowledge, credibility, and respect. And the old "screw your way to the top" was no longer in vogue as it might have been perceived to be 25 years ago. Give them what they needed, like their male counterparts, and they would take it from there, thank you.

Were they physically attractive? He thought so to a certain extent. But with where he was in his life, he was more attracted to what was between a woman's ears. While it was completely out of context, he recalled Jack Nicholson's outlandishly sexist commentary in A Few Good Men that included the line: "There is nothing on this earth sexier, believe me gentleman, than a woman you have to salute early in the morning."[1]

There had been many prospects and opportunities but in addition to his commitment to his marriage vows, even before he was married he had stayed away from office romance. He had actually applied his considerable analytic abilities to examine the Pro's and Con's on this topic and determined there were very few positives to be had in dating a business associate. Recalling his political science university studies, he had distilled the issue down to the relationship version of the separation of church and state, and arrived at "the separation of business and pleasure". He had determined that the vast majority of these romances were more physical than emotional and the awkwardness, embarrassment, endless "covert activity" planning, and even exposure to harassment claims overwhelmingly outweighed any emotional and physical pleasure derived from such a relationship.

---

1. *A Few Good Men*, Castle Rock Entertainment 1992

This aspect of his moral code had not kept his wife from questioning him about his late nights and "on the road" activities. Regardless of his innocence and his clear understanding of his wife's motivation — her love for him; her insecurity about her physical appearance; and her feeling that she was out of touch with the industry since her retirement 8 years ago — the conversations were still uncomfortable for him. He was sure they were for her, as well.

Denise was a very attractive woman. While he still considered her hot, she was 40 hot not 25 hot, in her mind. He preferred the 40 hot, but knew that no level or length of discussion would convince her of that.

Brains had always influenced his view of beauty, so much so that it was exactly that quality that had moved him from a casual notice of his wife 15 years ago at an industry conference, to a fiery, lust-filled courtship, and eventually marriage. She was beautiful and bright and he had been smitten with her from the first. She had continued to work as a marketing executive for a number of years after they married, but had retired after the birth of their second child to focus on the homefront.

Sure, he thought, kids, life, work, and everything had intervened and maybe the fire wasn't what it used to be, but he still loved her, and still lusted for her. He couldn't envision a life in which they were not partners, friends, and lovers.

With all that well understood in his pained and wet state, he noted that this line of thinking was coming to top-of mind status more frequently. Something was not right, not really wrong, but just not right. What exactly wasn't right, wasn't clear.

He was a golfer. No, duffer was a more accurate description. But he played frequently enough and understood the game to the extent that he could draw parallels between the game and life. His understanding of the game was also limited to the extent that while he could see his shots could be off just a little (pretty frequently), he had trouble identifying **what** was off. He felt the same way about his marriage — he was a "low-handicap husband", which was pretty damn good, but wasn't sure what he needed to change to have a "scratch" marriage, which would be VERY good. If this were a business process he would say it was not "optimized". They weren't going to break-up or anything like that, but things had room for improvement.

He knew it.

And he knew that she knew it.

Every once in a while he even let her know that he knew.

His time spent at work was becoming a more frequent topic of conversation. And the conversation would often swing from the emotional extreme of groundless claims of infidelity to the more practical end of work / life balance. Invariably he would agree to what he knew was an unachievable commitment to re-balance his life, spend more time with her and the kids, and recapture that flame between them by focusing on them as a couple.

He really wanted to make good on the commitment, but he had other obligations. The old saying in his company was that you only had to work half-days, and you got to choose which 12 hours they were. It had been that way when he joined the company and it would be that way when he finally decided he had enough— whenever that would be.

That had also been a recent source of tension. "When would it end?" she had asked. Not that the company had not paid him well. But there was an attraction, no, more of an addiction, that the money had created for both material and experiential things. They hadn't lived above their means, a common problem with many of their friends. But they had fallen prey to social pressure to acquire material goods that were not needed.

He flashed on the phrase he had heard as a young boy "Keeping up with the Jones' ". As a child he had always wondered who the Jones family was and what kind of race it was. As he got older he found out that there weren't any Jones' per se. They were the Williams', the Franklins, the Smiths, and others. While there may be great value to copying others' ideas of comfort, recreation, and consumer product functionality, when the motive moved from actual personal need values to a "me too" , they had entered into the ugly zone. Car, house, appliances, club memberships, clothing, jewelry, and sporting equipment—the list was endless.

Had they gotten in so deep that they had become the Jones'? Had the new acquisitions of their friends or acquaintances become a "must have" simply to gain social acceptance? Whatever the answers were, their financial good fortune had influenced them and allowed them to be sucked into the image game—a game that required a significant entrance fee and continuing financial maintenance.

Should he, or could he, exit the game?

Another body shot of pain brought him to the conclusion that there was nothing that the reflection on his social standing and his relationship with his wife was going to do to help him now.

"Focus!" he thought again, but his normally disciplined mind was not following his instruction. He just needed to find his cell phone and dial 911. Of course maybe he also needed some light and a functioning leg to find that cell phone.

The fact that the sun had set at 7:00 p.m. and the accelerated darkness created by the storm had influenced the series of events that led to his current circumstances was completely lost on him. The possibility that he could have avoided all of this by having left work at a decent hour, never entered his scrambled mind.

Roses!

As he assessed his surroundings he thought he smelled roses. He couldn't be entirely sure as he wasn't really sure of anything at this point. It had been so long since he had seen his yard in daylight during the work week that he had finally succumbed to the need to have his moderately talented gardeners take over the duties of caring for his flower garden and his prize-winning roses.

Roses!

Cut roses from his garden. There was something so beautiful and natural about them. And it was something that he had created. And they were always met with a smile…her smile.

His wife's smile seemed to be more with her eyes than her lips when he presented her with a bouquet of roses from the garden. Her eyes could cut right through him. She seemed to see everything in him: The Good, The Bad, and The Ugly. Sometimes he had the feeling that she was clairvoyant. Or she was just so intuitive and skilled in the area of interpersonal relationships that she influenced her environment to the point of making things happen the way she wanted. And while he sensed that "just not right" feeling about the relationship, he knew he could still get that smile going: Roses.

Yep, head out to the garden and cut a "bouquet-on-demand." Yep, he needed to do that. When was the last time he had done that? When was the last time he had seen that smile? He so wanted to see that smile now.

When would he see it?

When would she get there?

★   ★   ★

CHAPTER II
MEMORY LANE

CRACK! The sharp sound startled him and brought him back to his immediate reality.

"Hey Tom! Tommy? Tommy Boy? You Big Stud!"

"What the Hell?!" he mumbled as he became conscious that his surroundings now included a rather husky female voice.

"Well there we are," the voice said, as his eyes slowly opened. "It's about time you woke up. You must have really banged your head when you missed that curve earlier."

"Missed the curve?! I was driven off the road!" Tom

replied as his sight had been fully restored and he gazed upon a scantily clad figure that looked to be a cross between Jennifer Aniston and Sharon Stone: strong, sexy, confident of her attractiveness, and undeniably a woman accustomed to being in control. "Who the hell are you? How'd you get down here?"

"Oh Tommy Tommy Tommy! I was just about to ask you the exact same questions: Who the hell are you, really; and how did you end up being here?

"Tell you what I am going to do. Now that you're awake, I am going to help answer those questions for you and with you 'cuz that dumbfounded look on your face isn't giving me any confidence that you can answer them by yourself. And by the way, that is not your most attractive look and we both know your vanity quotient, right?

"Where is that damn cell phone?" she said in *his* voice. "An interesting question, but not one we should really care about right now. I'm going to take you on a little voyage to a place "a long time ago, in a galaxy far, far away," she said now in a perfect imitation of Obi-Wan Kenobi of Star Wars fame. Our trip will take us back in time to help you better understand who you are and how you got here."

"I can save us both some time and tell you how I got here! Like I said before, it was that damn driver that cut across the road and almost hit me head-on. But never mind that, who the hell are you? And why aren't you wet from the rain?"

"Still a little cocky and controlling, Tommy? Well, while a little annoying at times, that was always part of your charm," her tone coming across like an ex-lover with fond memories of times past. "My name is Love."

"Love? That's a good one. How about you show me some *love* and get me the hell out of here?" Tom demanded.

With her patience wearing thin, an emotional switch was flipped. Love had had enough and shifted to a combination of School Marm and Dominatrix. "OK. Time to level set, Tommy Boy! It's time for you to stow the attitude where the sun doesn't shine. You need a friend and from what I can see, I am the only option currently available. So how about you stop acting like a little spoiled brat and consider me a friend who is here to give you what you need," she replied. Despite her frustration with her charge, she started singing.

"No, you can't always get what you want.

No, you can't always get what you want.

No, you can't always get what you want.

But if you try sometime, you just might find,

You get what you need."[2]

"Spoiled Brat?! What I need?! I need to get out of here, that's what I need! You have a cell phone? Can you call 911? Call my wife? Can you get somebody here to help me?"

"Tommy," she laughed. "I *am* here to help you. In the world of beggars and choosers, right now you are the poorest of beggars. So how about you change your tone and more importantly get focused on the right questions? And just to let you know, where I come from there are no cell phones, at least not yet."

Whether it was fatigue or mental failure, Tom succumbed to the realization that whatever was going on

---

2. Chorus from The Rolling Stones' song "You Can't Always Get What You Want" ©1969 by Mick Jagger and Keith Richards.

was not going to improve by his continued protestation. He was a gifted communicator with a significant arsenal of approaches to deploy in verbal battles against any adversary. But the combined effects of the accident and his concussion-induced imagination, had transformed him into an unarmed man in the battle of wits with this vixen. He decided to just let it happen and go where his imagination was taking him.

"Tommy? You still with me, Buddy?"

"Quit calling me Tommy!" he demanded.

"We all called you Tommy back then. I know you got a bang on the head, but don't you remember? That's what we had to call you if we ever expected to get a call back from you.

"I know you must be confused, so to be very clear Tommy, I am not a figment of your imagination as much as I am an amalgamation or representation of your past, your past friends, your past lovers, and your past conquests. Tommy, I am here to help you as you say 'get outta here', and to help you understand where 'HERE' really is. For you to really understand that, you need to visit that which has come before, when we were both younger.

"Can you remember when life was simpler? When we had all the answers? Do you recall when we couldn't spell the word 'consequences' and 'responsibility' was a four letter word?"

Making no progress towards reconciling Love's words and his current reality, Tom tried to take in this creature and really see what he was up against. It certainly appeared that he had the time.

One thing was for certain, his imagination still had it. Whomever or whatever Love was, she was the perfect female specimen: intelligent and sharp-witted, with an athletic wholesomeness balanced with a hint of sluttiness. Her more than ample, and partially visible breasts were perfectly matched to a nicely rounded and firm backside. While this bizarre experience was clearly not setting up to be a sexual fantasy, if it had gone in that direction, she could easily have been the object of his affection. And she was right in one respect: she was the representation of the best aspects of all the girls he had ever dated, both physically and mentally. The jury was still out on her attitude.

Love was an interesting cocktail: casual, sophisticated, classy, sweet, and tough. And all that Love was seemed to be revealing itself in the brief time Tom had spent with her.

She now reached out to offer her hand to him. It was a soft yet strong hand, not decorated with jewelry, yet enhanced with a simple and elegant manicure.

Tom protested, " I can't get up. Between my head and my leg I can't go anywhere. And besides, you aren't real anyway."

She laughed, "Tommy. Tommy. Tommy. Your perspective of 'real' is about to change. Are age and stress catching up with you? Getting up never used to be a problem for you back in the day. That was always one of your more attractive qualities.

"C'mon, Big Boy," she said as she proceeded to reach down and around Tom's body. Finding his derriere, she gave it a massive squeeze. Instantly Tom no longer felt the pain from his injuries or the rain and cold. He was also astonished that he was now standing straight up and could now see that she was every inch as tall as his 6 foot height.

"OK," Tom thought to himself. "Let's give *this* a shot.

Focus!" as he tested his level of consciousness one last time by slapping himself across his face to see if he would wake up.

"Feel better?"' Love asked.

"OK, now I know I am completely messed up. What the hell, since I am apparently not going to wake up from this soon, I'll roll with this," Tom conceded. "So now are you gonna remind me of all the girls I dated? Should I start responding to the name Ebenezer? Am I going to get to repent my ways and save Tiny Tim? Give gifts to the poor? And your real name, is it Ghost of Lovers Past?"

"More questions Tommy?" she chuckled. "And still the wrong ones! But welcome aboard. You're starting to catch on. We're going to embark upon our 'date' in a moment, but just to give you a heads-up, after I show you the town, I'll be sharing you with a couple of my friends, Carin and Liv. They'll be helping you complete your journey in a little while. But more about them later. So you ready for your little trip down memory lane?"

"Fine. Bring it on, Love!" he stated with a very poor English accent. "I'll role with it but I don't get what's in it for me. I've already been there, right? And as I recall, it was a pretty unremarkable past."

"You know, that the bump on your head may have affected your memory. But I'll provide more context and clarity for you. To be honest, there was quite a lot that went on that was pretty interesting. In fact yours has been a *very* remarkable life that resulted in your being here today," she started to explain until Tom protested, feeling a surge of strength and confidence from the effects of her earlier touch.

"I told you! It was that damn…"

"Enough!" she roared with a very deep and powerful tone, the Marm-Matrix flashing back. "OK, Tommy Boy. Listen up! God gave you two ears and one mouth and it is now time that you started using them in that proportion. No more cars. No more accidents. You are here due to a series of events that have led you here. It's that simple, capiche? My friends and I are going to provide you with the opportunity to truly understand how your life has been shaped by your past, the current state of affairs, and what the future may hold for you.

"This awareness may change your life. I say 'may' because what you do from here is entirely your choice, short-term and long-term. You can choose to have an open mind, take advantage of the situation, and learn something or you can be that spoiled brat I've been listening to for the last 10 minutes who thinks he knows everything. Your call, but I strongly suggest that for the next little while you just sit back and enjoy, Tommy.

"To be honest, Big Fella, you have no choice. Remember the TV reruns you liked as a boy, the Outer Limits?" she asked.

With this second reference to science fiction, he wondered how she knew of his liking for this genre, a fascination that had never waned to this day. He attempted to respond only to find that his ability to speak had suddenly vanished.

"We will control what you see and hear," she said with the exact same voice as the announcer had in the 1960's television show.

Returning to the Sweet Love version she continued, "And Tommy, I will also let you know when it's time for you to be heard. Until you start to catch on to the REAL difference between cause and effect, let's just play like you are at a private screening of an old movie starring characters with which you have a great familiarity."

With that Love grabbed his right elbow with the force of a prize fighter's punch. He instinctively winced, anticipating what he thought was going to be a painful shot up his arm, and squeezed his eyes shut hoping that in his temporary blindness, he would not experience the impending pain.

A silent, momentary chuckle arose in him as he wondered how often he had shut his eyes to avoid pain. "If you can't see it, it can't hurt you," he thought to himself. Avoidance of pain had always been an objective in his life.

Ironically, it was never the physical pain that really impacted him. To the contrary, Tom had frequently put himself in situations in which he knew he would feel significant physical pain. He had trained himself to view it as just another sensation like touch or smell, and had an incredibly high threshold for it.

But the emotional side of his life was a different story. At the slightest hint of mental anguish he had reacted in accordance with the old emergency safety training from childhood: duck and cover. Avoidance and escape. And he had mastered techniques for emotional protection just as well as he had done to tolerate physical discomfort.

As soon as it started, his attempt at self-analysis came to an abrupt end as he noticed that Love's touch was curiously not painful, and clearly something over which he had absolutely no control. He was puzzled by the familiar effect of this contact, a repeat of the sensation he had experienced as she had raised him to his feet a few minutes earlier. And now it hit him: her touch had the same effect as the pre-op "happy shot" he had enjoyed with his numerous orthopedic procedures. In the preparation process for general anesthesia, the shot always resulted in a euphoric state which removed any anxiety he had about the upcoming surgery.

Unbeknownst to Tom, that was exactly the state of mind that was necessary for him to have for what he was about to experience.

★ ★ ★

With the danger having passed, he opened his eyes but instantly felt a jolt that forced him to close them again.

It was the sun.

"What the hell!" he thought. Love's ability to enable Tom to stand on the rainy slope below the road was something, but this was an even better trick.

He blinked his way to opening his eyes and quickly discovered he was no longer on that slope. He was no longer in the rain. He was standing by a swimming pool. A broad smile took over Tom's face as he recognized where he was: the Alpine Oaks Country Club.

> *"Ball Up!" his eldest brother Billy commanded. A seven year old Tom Daniels immediately complied by bringing his knees to his chest and tightly grasping his hands around his shins. The technique in assuming the form of a ball in the pool was not only well-honed but executed with a willingness and excitement that indicated what was about to happen was something he was really looking forward to.*
>
> *As Tom "assumed the position", his brother, 8 years his senior, caught him before he began to sink in the water. He proceeded to position his 'ball' on his shoulder with his hands expertly placed underneath it. He then threw it up in the air toward his partner in this game of human catch, the 3rd Daniels brother Jordy, age 13.*
>
> *Distance, height, and accuracy were the objectives of the older boys as they repeated the process again and again. Regardless of their success, the wide smile and uncontrollable laughter of their little brother indicating his total enjoyment was always the result.*

Love looked at Tom, noting that his smile has not

really changed much in 37 years. She also could see that the reluctance in Tom to experience his past had vanished.

SPLAT!

Little Tommy had just violated one of the cardinal rules of "Ball Up" by prematurely releasing his hold on his legs in mid-air resulting in a very loud and painful back flop on the water.

Tom winced as though he was back in the pool himself.

"Wow! That was a good one," laughed Billy as he gathered up his temporarily paralyzed little brother.

"Hey Tommy, do that again," yelled Jordy. "Billy throw him way up there this time!"

"You OK?" a widely grinning Billy asked his little brother, with just a hint of concern.

"I'm fine," lied Tommy as he endured the painful effects of his mistake. "Let's go!" he said as he knew that if he told his brother he was hurting, whether for fear of parental reprisal or genuine caring, his complaint could lead to a break in the game. Any pause in the action could lead to a premature end to the game and little Tom was not about to be the cause of that. Pain or no pain, there was nothing more fun than being his brothers' playmate and he would do anything and everything in his power to continue.

"C'mon, let's go," demanded Tommy.

"OK. Ball up!" Billy directed and into the air Tommy went again.

Tom and Love watched this for a while, observing the various spins, trajectories, and landings that the brothers executed with their ball. Observing Tom's reaction to all this, Love wasn't sure which Tom was having more fun.

"Good times?" she asked.

"The best," Tom replied.

"Man, the things those guys did to me!" he reflected. "But you know, they could have tortured me and I would have asked for more. In fact, as I think about it, they did torture me a fair amount, and I did ask for more. Anything to be with them— to be included. And I just remember laughing. I'm talking total uncontrollable, hurting-stomach-muscles, pee-in-your-pants laughter when I was with those guys."

"You really loved them, huh?" she asked.

"Ya think! I'm not sure that I thought of it in those terms back then. I just knew that there was nothing better than playing with them and I would do anything to be part of whatever they were doing.

"They were my idols. They were great athletes, had all sorts of great friends who would always come by the house, and as I recall, always had very pretty girl friends. I'm not sure that I wanted to be like them when I grew up, I just know that I wanted to be around them when I was a kid.

"And they were pretty good about including me in the things they were doing, even beyond the regular Ball-up game. It didn't matter what I was doing, if I heard them calling my name, I was there."

*   *   *

As Tom closed his eyes, totally lost in his fond memories, Love firmly grabbed his elbow again and turned him around.

He opened his eyes to find he was still at a pool, but no longer at the informal setting of the country club he had been enjoying with his brothers. The playful noise of the recreational pool had been replaced by the murmuring of a crowd of people, the intermittent shouting and whistling of coaches providing direction, the crack of the starter's gun, and the unmistakable monotonous sound made by people's arms slapping the water as they swam in a pool…a sound he had heard for many years, many years ago. And there was that unforgettable scent of chlorinated water.

He was at a goddamn swim meet! How many of these had he attended in his life…as a swimmer, a coach and a parent? Too many and not enough. He felt the rush of a whole different set of memories and emotions come flooding into his mind.

As he soaked in his new environment, he also took the opportunity to take a long look at Love. She was standing next to him. He had been so immediately sucked into the fun with his brothers that he hadn't taken notice of her in the light. She was very beautiful in a natural way. In addition to her physical appearance, she had a presence about her that was overwhelmingly attractive. Why hadn't he married 'her'? Or had he?

The two of them were there, but just like their visit to the Brothers Daniels' game, nobody seemed to recognize their presence. Not that anyone would have necessarily noticed him, but Tom was sure that if the rest of the people there saw Love, the proceeding would have come to a screeching halt.

"Ladies and Gentlemen, we would like to direct your attention to the awards stand. We are now presenting the awards for the Boys 10 and under 100 Butterfly. Our winner, in a new California State Record Time, is Tom Daniels!" A significant round of applause followed, causing the young boy (Tom, some 34 years younger) at the top step of the awards stand to blush from the attention.

After a brief photo session, the 10-year old Tommy leaped off the award stand and ran over to a very welcoming group of fans: his parents; his team mates; and his coach, brother Billy. And while all of the adulation was fun, Tommy had something else on his mind—getting back to the lively card game of Spades that he and his buddies John, Wes, Jeff, and Richie had been engaged in before being interrupted by the awards ceremony. After all, he was a 10 year old kid and had his priorities.

A copy of a newspaper suddenly appeared in Tom's hand.

"Daniels sets State Record at Junior Olympics Swim Meet" was the small headline in the local paper's sports section.

Tom's mind was filled with the memories of the crowd cheering, the endless hours practicing, and the sacrifices in his personal life that kept him away from what most of the kids got to do. But he also remembered that he thoroughly enjoyed every minute of all of it. He smiled as he reflected on the respect he received from others, young and old, for his accomplishments.

He also reflected on the finite aspect of the sport of swimming which, like some other individual sports, was a battle against the clock. It was always a contest against the water and the stopwatch (the analog device now only seen on the television news show "60 Minutes", that was used before digital timers and touchpads became ubiquitous). Winning was nice, but the goal was always the P.R.—the Personal Record.

It wasn't just the races and the socializing and camaraderie associated with practices and swim meets that stuck out in his mind. It was the time. It was the endless hours with his friends and brothers. He recalled spending what seemed to be every waking hour at the "club" and other swimming venues. It was his life as a youngster and it had been a blast.

And with all the positives that had come from his competitive swimming experience: the physical conditioning; knowledge of the sport and the physics and techniques associated with it; mental discipline; the correlation between hard work and success; and the recognition of his accomplishments, Tom's mind arrived at one question: How great would another game of *Ball Up* be?

Tom's eyes started to well up. He was not sure whether it was from the memory of a simpler time filled with fun, love, and positive achievements, void of the pressures of his current life, or the vivid memory of swimming in highly chlorinated water before swimming goggles became a standard for all swimmers. As he reached up to rub his eyes, he again felt the soothing touch of Love's hand on his arm and the sensation of movement without any effort on his part.

"Time to move again, Love?" he thought to himself.

*   *   *

Tom's hands dropped from his eyes to reveal that he was now indoors in his family's home, viewing himself, or the 13 year old version of himself, stretched out on a couch watching television. While he would have probably chastised his own kids for wasting time like this in front of the tube, pelting them with questions about the status of their chores and homework, he knew *his* situation had been different.

Back then, Tom's daily schedule for the standard week had consisted of 5:00 am swim practice, followed by school, homework, 2 more hours of swim practice and finishing homework. He also had managed to fit in an interest in girls along the way but did not have much time to spend with them, much less, learn to develop a deep relationship with them.

He wondered what his kids, Brad and Jamie, thought of their lives and the structure he and his wife Denise, had imposed on them. Had he ever asked? Did he know what they thought about anything? And if he did ask, did he *really* listen to their replies?

But the past drew him back. As he became more oriented to his surroundings he saw that the show on the television was a rebroadcast of the old original Star Trek show. He reacted immediately and sharply, "C'mon! Really?! OK, Love! Do I have to do this? We both know what this is and I can't see what purpose is going to be served by reliving it," he said.

"The good with the bad, Tommy Boy. The good with

the bad," she said.

The phone rang in the house, prompting the younger version of Tom to rise up from the couch to answer it. The voice at the other end introduced itself as "Stanford Hospital" and asked to speak with Tom's father. "Dad, it's for you," he shouted as he placed the phone down, returned to the couch, and proceeded to re-engage with the crew of the Starship Enterprise.

Very quickly after getting on the phone, his father's face dropped and he hung up the phone.

"There's been an accident. It's Billy and it doesn't look good."

Tom got up and turned down the volume on the television, hoping to hear the conversation between his parents in the other room. While he couldn't hear any of the specifics, his mother's crying confirmed to him that his father's assessment was an understatement.

As his parents swept through the kitchen on their way to the garage and the car, Tom was told to not worry.

"Just stay off the phone and we will call you as soon as we know something," his mother told him.

No phone call ever came.

2 hours passed until he heard the garage door open, signaling that his parents had returned. Tom got up from the couch, expecting to see his parents and his brother enter from the garage door.

He hadn't even considered the reality that he was hit with when his father and mother entered the house alone.

"Bill is dead," his father announced in a sad but controlled way. "There was nothing they could do. His

injuries were just too severe. The only good news is that he passed away very quickly and didn't suffer."

Tom quickly learned that his eldest brother had been in the front passenger seat of a car being driven by one of his friends. Less than a mile away from their house, someone ran a red light and smashed into the car where Billy was sitting. He died from multiple internal injuries.

It didn't occur to the teenager Tom at the time, but over the years Tom would always think it strange that he was left home alone while his parents rushed to the hospital to see what had happened to his eldest brother. In hindsight it was something of a harbinger of a lingering sense of "alone" he would experience and seek to overcome for the following 30 some odd years.

Love stepped away from Tom as she observed her travel partner in a different light. Even with his involuntary submissiveness due to the control she possessed over him, she had not seen this side of him, now or back in the day. She observed this powerful man in a totally deflated state. He did not appear defeated but just empty.

Any person that had gotten to know Tom at all knew about the death of his eldest brother, and that included all the women that made up Love. She knew that it had contributed to what made him strong both physically and emotionally. But it also had served to expose and create some flaws.

Tom's brother had been his hero. An All-American athlete, a personality as big as all outdoors, and a father figure, his brother had been a kind of replacement for a real father who traveled extensively. His father had not been a bad Dad by any means, but his brother's availability and the eight-year difference in their ages, combined to elevate his brother's status. It was a status Billy never sought, nor lived long enough to realize.

"Wound still open?" she asked

"Which one?"

"The loss of your brother."

"Actually the pain of that event was addressed and subsided pretty quickly. It was all the other bullshit that followed that still hurts. Someone told me once that all families are dysfunctional, it's just a matter of degree. If that is true, our dysfunction quotient skyrocketed that January evening of 1982."

Love allowed an awkward silence to play out until Tom felt the need to end it.

"I know that family members die. It is inevitable. Nobody escapes a lifetime alive. But when they die at 21, the coping difficulty factor for the surviving family members goes up substantially. When the family member is a father-figure, a hero both for their own accomplishments and for being a coach of one's burgeoning athletic career, the word devastating starts kicking in. And when an adolescent doesn't identify with an emotional role model, get ready for an emotional basket case world. When I read about it in my college psych classes, I thought somebody had done a white paper on me.

"There's more," Tom stated, seeming to hold Love responsible for the events he had just relived. "You want more? How much do you want to turn the knife?"

"Wow,"Love responded. "I'm sorry for your loss Tom. I know there is some heavy stuff in there. Well I guess you've earned yourself a free pass from having to re-live all of the fun associated with this part of your life."

Tom didn't respond to Love's failed attempt at humor.

*   *   *

Tom shook his head and looked down until he was revived by the unmistakable smell that he hadn't experienced for years—the post-beer bust scent of his college fraternity house.

"Oh God!" he gasped. "What the hell are we doing here? I know you said that there may be some of my past that had value I might not recall. But I can assure you that outside of the friendships formed here, my time in this house could not be considered valuable!"

"Well Tommy," Love responded. "I think that concussion of yours may be impacting the ol' memory more than you thought. Walk with me," she commanded as she led him out to the front veranda of the House.

There, sitting in a pair of comfortable, over-stuffed and very worn chairs, was Tom's brother Jordy and a long-haired, 20 year old Tom on a beautiful warm early afternoon in Los Angeles.

"Oh man! Jordy at my fraternity house. That was a pretty interesting occurrence, given how straight he was," Tom recalled.

> *"You wanna a beer?" Tom asked his brother.*
>
> *"It's a little early for me. You having one?" Jordy asked.*
>
> *"Having one? I NEED one! Last night was pretty crazy. You want one or not?" Tom impatiently asked again.*

"Sure," Jordy responded, reluctantly accepting the offer but having absolutely no interest in actually drinking it at 2:00pm in the afternoon.

As Tom headed up to his room to get a couple of Buds from his mini-fridge, he racked his mind for what he was actually going to talk about with his brother. Having not spent much time with Jordy over the last 7 years, he really didn't know his older brother very well. "This is going to be fun," he thought sarcastically.

As he returned to the cluttered patio with the beer he said, "So how are things?"

"Going pretty well," Jordy said. "Working my ass off but things are good. You?"

"Good. Mom & Dad ok?"

"Yeah, they're ok. Mom is still a little off. She hasn't been the same since Billy died. But I guess none of us have been the same since then."

"Well it happened and we have to get on with our lives," Tom responded rather matter-of-factly.

"Really? That simple? Just move on?" Jordy responded almost too quickly. He started thinking that he might need to be asking for something a little stronger than the warming beer in his hand.

"What are you going to do? What can you do? There's nothing that is going to bring him back."

"Of course there isn't, but doesn't it still hurt?" Jordy asked. "I dunno, it's not for me to tell you how to act or feel. Maybe I was just closer to him because of our closeness in age."

"What the hell does that mean?! I didn't care? I wasn't close to him because of our age difference? How the hell would you know? He was still at home with me *and you were off at school when he died," Tom responded with an increasing level of aggravation and defensiveness about where the conversation was going.*

"I know, but you never seemed to care that much. Everyone was losing it and you just sat there."

"Well screw you! Who appointed you judge and jury?! You came all the way down to L.A. from Davis to tell me that I didn't love my brother? Gimme a friggin' break!" Tom shouted.

"I'm not saying you didn't care about him, but I never saw you show any emotion. I don't think I ever saw you even cry once through the whole thing. At the funeral or ever. It just always seemed strange to me."

Tom watched the conversation from the past unfold and began to shake in unison with his 20 year old image, until a calming hand from Love brought him down.

"Look, you weren't there seeing Mom balling her eyes out every night at dinner. You weren't there seeing Dad being the unfeeling asshole that he is. I was 13 and I made a choice: suck it up. It wasn't very easy for me. I dealt with and deal with it in my own way, and it seemed that while I copied the Old Man, you don't seem to think I acted appropriately. Ask me if I care?"

Tom's beer was gone and without explanation he abruptly got up to get another.

Upon his return, Jordy spoke a little less judgmentally, "OK OK. I'm sorry. I didn't make the trip down here to give you shit. I just thought that since I was here for business, I'd stop by and say hi. As I drove over here, I got to thinking that we've never discussed his death. We talked about him, but not what happened afterward. To be honest, I've been a little pissed at you about the way you reacted. I didn't think you gave a shit. Maybe I sold you a little short on that one," Jordy conceded, offering an olive branch.

After a long silence, Tom said, *"I gave a shit, but didn't know what to do, except follow Dad's example. Why? I dunno…but it seemed better than what Mom was going through. Hell I was 13. You didn't think I cared? For 7 fucking years?!!"*

"I'm sorry," Jordy repeated after taking a long draw from his now warm beer. *"You gotta another one of these?"*

Tom appeared reflective as he connected this conversation with his current relationship with his older brother. There was no question that the 13 year old and 19 year old siblings had reacted differently to the tragic death of their brother. Right or wrong, they had done what they each thought was right and in their best interest.

And as awkward and angry as the conversation had been those many years ago, two very positive things had come from it. First, the genesis of Tom's belief that grieving and reaction to tragedy was a personal choice, not to be judged by others. Regardless of the approach with which you identify, religiously or scientifically- based, very simply, people need to be provided the freedom to deal with things in the way that feels right for them. Some need solitude to cope, others will have a need to not be alone and seek help from others.

Whatever the personal choices, Tom felt the path through the grieving process is always best decorated by support, not judgment.

The second result of this unlikely yet timely bro-meeting was that it formed the basis for his becoming much closer to his brother Jordy. Over the years the two brothers' relationship had evolved to a point where they did discuss their personal issues with one another, had become far more connected and regularly socialized with their families. They had become good friends. The old saying 'you can't choose your relatives' notwithstanding, Tom felt fortunate to have Jordy as his brother and given the opportunity, would have chosen him. How many people in his life was he that close to? Outside of his wife Denise, he couldn't think of one.

Tom's face changed to present a kind of let-me-count-my-blessings smile as he compared this event to the annual presentation of the William Daniels Memorial Scholarship Award that he and Jordy jointly awarded at their hometown high school. The event was their homage to their brother and touched on their memories of his spirit, humor, and accomplishment. They presented the award in a way that celebrated Bill's spirit, with a particular emphasis on the humor, making it the highlight of the annual awards ceremony.

Tom thought about the portion of the presentation in which after sharing the story about his brother Bill, he would lift the audience's spirits by stating, "Bill left us many years ago, but he is still here with that bright smile of his. He returns with us to award this scholarship every year."

He wondered whether there was something more important at work in that sentence than just turning what could be perceived as a sad story into something more positive. Did he truly believe in the spiritual presence of his late brother? Did Bill really make an appearance every year? Or was it a form of denial—a coping mechanism that had lingered and been leveraged all these years.

Both Jordy and Tom had experiences that suggested some form of non-physical communication truly existed. Jordy had shared with Tom a recurring dream he had after Bill's death that suggested Bill's lingering spiritual presence. He had envisioned their late brother on the other side of a fence that separated the swimming pool area of the Alpine Oaks Country Club from the San Francisquito Creek, which separated the Club from the bordering, undeveloped land of Portola Valley. In the dream, Jordy waved and shouted encouragement to Billy to come over the fence to join him, to which Jordy received the saddening response, "I can't."

Regardless of how Tom had held his emotions inside in dealing with his brother's death and initially viewed the events in an absolute way—dead/gone— he truly believed Bill did indeed stop by periodically, to check in on him.

The first occurrence had been unsettling as he experienced the physical sensation of some spirit moving through, and for a moment lingering, in his body. After that initial experience the *visits* became something he did not fear. He now welcomed, and thoroughly enjoyed, the visits. He only wished he could control the timing of their occurrences and could establish a communication that extended beyond just the presence.

"Where was he now?" he wondered.

"Ya know," Tom said aloud, assessing the more relaxed conversation he was still observing between the two brothers sharing a fresh beer at the fraternity house, "that may have been the best argument I ever had."

The brothers Daniels had come a long way since then, he thought.

All three of them.

*   *   *

"God I hope you have had enough of this because I certainly have. Although I must say Jordy and I have been much closer since that conversation," Tom commented, still reflecting on his relationship with both his brothers.

"See? I told you: the good with the bad, Tommy. There are just a couple of places left for me to take you. They represent what might be your greatest weakness and the beginning of your greatest achievement."

Love couldn't tell whether he heard her or not. Tom had slipped into a deeper reflective stupor after moving past the inventory of his friendship with Jordy. He had settled in on an examination of the what might have been's (had Bill lived) and the what the hell is going on's (his late brother's spiritual visits).

He knew that there really was nothing to be gained by the fantasy-based exercise of projecting what life would be like had his brother not died that night. But it was almost irresistible to fantasize about the possibilities.

What was very fascinating to Tom, however, were the questions around Bill's visits. Why did they occur? Was there a way to understand a greater purpose or value from them? While he felt that these were more legitimate thoughts than those about the denial-based what-if's, these spiritual questions seemed just as unanswerable.

"Play Ball!!" Love yelled with a voice reminiscent of the home plate umpire from the old Candlestick Park stadium in San Francisco that he had visited as a child going to San Francisco Giants games. She then spun the startled Tom around and he was suddenly looking in a mirror. The reflection was of the 26 year old version of Tom. It wasn't a pretty picture — rough around the edges didn't begin to describe the image in the mirror.

At 26, his eyes were those of a 60 year old, swollen and bloodshot from what appeared to be a lack of sleep the night before. His cheeks were saturated by the failed attempts of his shaking hands to administer the morning dosage of Visine, to "get the red out." The volume of breath freshening liquid he was downing suggested a dual objective: freshen the breath and consume the trace amounts of alcohol in the concoction—a little "hair of the dog" that had clearly bitten him the night before. All of this appeared to be a well thought-out and practiced ritual.

Love looked at Tom. His eyes were now closed, so she gave him a little flick to the ear to get his attention, "You can't avoid it Tommy Boy. It's what you were."

"What I am!" Tom interrupted. "What I am! Once a drunk, always a drunk. But I do appreciate the reminder," he stated sarcastically, as he slowly, submissively blinked his eyes back to the scene before him.

"Now hold on Tom. As I said weakness AND achievement."

The image in the mirror appeared to finish his ritual by splashing his face with water and drying it with the paper towels from the office restroom. The image, of Tom less 18 years, appeared to be ready for whatever he was preparing for and gave himself one last evaluation. However negative the assessment, it was aligned to his immediate objective.

Tom left the restroom, walked down the hallway and stopped outside of an office with the sign, "Peggy Johnson, Human Resources Manager."

"OK. It took me a second but this is September 4th, isn't it?" Tom asked. Love did not respond as they both knew the answer.

Young Tom knocked on the door and was asked in. "Hi Peggy, gotta minute?"

"Well hello Tom, how are you today?" the 50-ish HR Manager responded with her signature greeting, designed to put all at ease and open up.

"I need help." Tom stated very directly. No question, just a statement of fact with an assumptive tone that Peggy was to be the provider of that help.

"Oh, so I see. No small talk today. What do you need help with?"

" Peggy, you know 'what with'. I've had it. I can't handle this. I have to stop drinking. I am still messed up from last night. I nearly killed myself in the car on the 405 last night. I just can't go on like this."

Tom paused as he briefly reflected on his unsuccessful 4-lane merge the night before that had resulted in his digging his car into a steep bank of ice plant.

"And it's not just that. It's now 5 to 6 nights a week. Some days I start at lunch. I just can't deal with this anymore." His head was bowed as he fessed-up to his activities and shared his feelings. He looked up at her with a blank face and furrowed brow, a vulnerable boy

and a beaten man.

"Got it," Peggy said with an understanding smile, knowing the ball was now in her court. She and Tom had had a few conversations about Tom's consumption and his increasingly frequent self-assessment of being a functioning alcoholic. She herself was 20 years sober and while she was careful not to impose her beliefs on anyone, she was just as careful to quickly respond to a cry for help from someone that so obviously needed it.

"OK....give me 10 minutes to make a few phone calls and come back," she said.

"Thanks," Tom nervously responded. While he knew this was absolutely the right thing to do, it was still a huge step for someone who had been drinking alcoholically for 8 years.

He had considered getting help many times before, but his old buddies Fear, Denial, and Booze had always joined forces to dissuade him.

Now he was ready.
Wasn't he?
Yes! He was ready!
And he was also very scared.

Tom joined the younger Tom in reflecting silently on the path that had led *them* to this moment. Tom had used his personal drive and energy after his brother's death to do very well in school and swimming, and to be accepted at a major university that also awarded him a swimming scholarship.

His accomplishments and recognition from friends and family fed young Tom's ego and provided him with both a sense of purpose and a feeling of being on top of the world. At least for a little while. 6 weeks after his high school graduation, a heart ailment that had been becoming increasingly symptomatic for a couple of years, led doctors at Stanford Hospital to provide him with 3 options: 1. Continue swimming and run the risk of a heart attack; 2. Have open heart surgery with no guarantee that the problem would be resolved; or 3. Stop all athletic activity and submit to drug therapy.

There was really only one option and the prize behind Door # 3 was chosen, more for him than by him. With the athletic carpet pulled out from under him, off he went to college, with quite a different approach and perspective than he had originally planned.

The school had been very gracious in allowing him to keep his scholarship for four years, something they had no obligation to do. He would work-off his scholarship by acting as an assistant coach and trainer for the team. His involvement with the athletic program, his team mates, and the entire university social scene that came with the environment was more than he had hoped for, an experience for which he was very grateful.

Yet the damage was done.

The downward spiral had begun.

He had proceeded to engage in all the activities that the disciplined life of a scholar-athlete does not allow. The best and worst that sex, drugs, and rock 'n roll could provide a college kid in Los Angeles in the late 1980's was experienced and experienced to the fullest. What he remembered of it was extraordinary. On the negative side of the frivolity was an increasing enjoyment for the taste of alcohol, a taste that progressed to over-use, abuse, and dependence.

Some suggest that what is gained from the university experience is split evenly between what happens in class and outside of it. He had long ago concluded that he probably tested that balance, but was able to function enough to earn a degree and gain from the academic experience.

The 26-year old Tom finished his latest cup of coffee, number 5 for the morning, when Peggy called him at his cubicle at 8:25 am. "Cool," he thought to himself. "10 minutes on the nose."

He met her in her office and was informed that all the insurance was handled and that the Employee Assistance Program provided for the appropriate counseling. "The local therapist for the program will see you Monday morning at 9:00 am," Peggy shared proudly.

"What? No! NOW! I need help NOW!" he shouted loudly.

"Calm down!" She scolded him. She stood and approached him to get him off his emotional ledge and hoped his outburst had not just outed his privacy to his co-workers outside of her office.

But he wasn't calming down. " If you don't get me some help before Monday, I will have tonight and the weekend to justify why this isn't a good idea. I guarantee I will not make it. I need help now!"

"Got it. Got it," she said. Wait for a second outside the door." She knew he was ready to get help and she needed to act before denial and rationalization returned and took control of him. She was not going to lose him.

It seemed that as soon as she closed the door behind him, she was calling him back in. "Here is the address. Dr. Santiago is waiting for you."

He thanked Peggy and held their friendly departing hug just a moment longer than usual.

He didn't know what exactly was going to happen, but he knew he was taking the first step toward something better. He had arrived painfully and luckily at that juxtaposition of weakness, pain, fear, yearning, clarity, and hope that some refer to as rock bottom. What spurred him to action that September day in 1995 were all the negatives, plus a dream of what life he could have sober and the hope that someone could help him.

"Nice," Tom said. That had been 17 years, 6 months, and 22 days ago, but who was counting. He knew that day had come to define him in so many ways and given him the strength and motivation to become the person he was and aspired to be.

Not that he was cured, but after nearly 20 years of sobriety he was a hell of a lot better than he was. While still leery of allowing himself too much of the non-drug induced highs life afforded, and always on guard to avoid the depths of life's lumps, he was pretty confident that for at least today he would not drink, and he appreciated not having the craving to do so.

While Love and Tom were whisked away with the 26-year old Tom down the 405 Freeway toward the small Orange County town of Laguna Niguel, California, Love observed the reflective side of Tom and chose to let it flow.

Tom became lost in the memories of his counseling sessions and group meetings, the "work", as it was referred to.

The introspection.

The honesty

The revelations.
The pain.
The emotion.
The time.
The reality.

What a phenomenal investment, he thought. He wondered what his life would be like if he had not made that trip that day.

"Thank God!" he whispered as he assessed everything that had changed, firmly believing that he would not be alive if not for that single decision and all that followed from it.

★   ★   ★

Love decided to cut short the visit with younger Tom after sensing the elder Tom's complete recall of his introduction to sobriety. She brought Tom back to reality by gently leading him through the front door of a restaurant. The location wasn't immediately evident to him, nor was the occasion, but whatever was taking place here was quite a celebration.

The music was blaring as they walked through what was usually the hostess area of the establishment and into the bar area. It was apparent that somebody had rented out the place as everyone seemed to know one another and was enjoying the party.

Adjacent to the bar was a dance floor, every inch of which was being utilized by a very happy and very inebriated group of people. The only thing that seemed strange to Tom was the fact that it appeared to be the middle of the afternoon.

"Why are all these people—Oh my God!" Tom caught himself mid-sentence as he finally got his bearings.

"The Marsden wedding. Now that was a serious party!" Tom shared with Love. "Johnny worked for The Cantina and they gave him a break on the booze so he and Liz decided to have their reception there. They closed The Cantina down for the entire Sunday afternoon. Not quite the kind of place I thought Liz would have wanted, but I think they were footing the bill, so there they were."

Love eased Tom over to the area past the dance floor where the restaurant's tables were set-up for the reception guests. Toward the left hand corner was a couple engaged in deep conversation.

"You feeling OK? You aren't looking too well," the attractive woman asked Tom Daniels.

This 28-year old version of Tom was quite different than the younger version Love and Tom had just watched head off to that first therapy session. He was very healthy looking and appeared to be in excellent physical condition, with the exception of the pale look on his face that had prompted his date's question.

"I dunno. I felt fine this morning, but maybe I'm coming down with something," Tom[28] responded. His girlfriend of 5 years, Marie, appeared as much perturbed as concerned.

"Oh great. Liz and Johnny finally tie the knot and you decide that you don't feel well. What's wrong?"

"I'm not sure. It's not like I have a cold or anything. I just feel real jittery, kind of antsy."

"Did you take your heart meds?" Marie asked, having seen the reaction Tom's body sometimes had if he had forgotten a dose.

"Yes, I did. I dunno what it is," Tom responded.

"C'mon, let's go dance," she suggested.

At that point, something changed in Tom, prompting him to let out a rather loud, "Holy Shit!"

"What?"

"I think I know what it is. I've been sober for 2 years right?" he said, not expecting an answer. "And before I quit, I used to head out in the afternoons and go to the local bars to start drinking. I gotta get outta here!" he exclaimed.

"Get ready for a lesson in sensitivity," Tom told Love

with a disgusted tone to his voice.

"You what? Why? We just got here!" protested Marie.

"I have to go," repeated Tom.

"Give me a break!" Marie replied. "We all know that you stopped drinking and say you are an alcoholic, but we've been in restaurants before and you've been OK. You never have a problem with me drinking in front of you when we're at home or when we go out. But now it's making you feel sick? Aren't you being a little dramatic here?"

"No. I don't think so and thanks for the support. It's 3 in the afternoon and I'm in a bar. I don't belong here. I could be wrong, but I don't want to deal with the consequences if I'm right and I slip."

"Oh so because you don't feel comfortable, I'm just supposed to get up and leave my best friend's wedding reception? I don't think so."

"Fine. You can stay and get a ride, but I gotta get outta here and now,' Tom explained.

"You're serious? Shit. Fine, then you go home, but I'm not going to offend Liz by leaving," Marie said as she grabbed her purse and margarita, leaving Tom alone at the table.

Tom sat at the table for a couple of minutes weighing his options. He knew he only had one. He looked around, found the back door and slid out without any goodbyes. He hoped that the happy couple would understand his situation and accept his apologies later, sensing that they were going to receive a less than accurate explanation of his departure from Marie.

Tom shook his head, feeling a sense of embarrassment from the memory of his relationship with Marie. "Funny how a clear mind can change your perspective on things," he said quietly to himself. Love saw no reason to interrupt what appeared to be the beginning of some productive introspection.

He was reminded of the decisions that he had made time and time again, including the one he made every day that he woke up…that he would not drink. And he thought of all the changes in his social habits and companions, and ultimately the end of the relationship with Marie, a woman with whom he thought he would build a life.

His sessions with Dr. S., his meetings, and his many conversations with others in the same boat always stressed the need to stay away from slippery places, those places that might lead one to fall off the wagon. It was a practice that Tom adopted and obsessively followed for many years. He had also heard about and experienced the process of losing almost every "friend" he had from his drinking days.

He recalled the tumultuous process of initially being respected for taking things in hand and making the decision to quit drinking. Then there was the experience of a mental and physical honeymoon period of excessive energy and excitement right after quitting, as his body and mind were cleansed of alcohol. He had even become somewhat of a celebrity amongst his friends, many of whom would ask him for his opinion and assessment of their personal situation with respect to over-imbibing in drugs and alcohol.

Tom was, and remained to this day, very cautious in providing advice. He respected the skill and training of professionals like Dr. S. and would always qualify his supportive comments by telling people that what he shared was only *his* experience, immediately followed by a suggestion that if they had doubts, they should seek the advice of a professional.

In time Tom started to experience a level of alienation as his growing success with recovery was viewed as a threat by many of his friends.

"You know, Love, I used to think that all those people I drank with were my friends until later when I realized that my time in the bars was really just a chance for me and the rest of the drunks to be 'alone together'. The booze fooled me into thinking there was something else happening, like friendship. I was just anesthetizing, not interacting."

"You ever miss it? Those friends?" she asked.

"The booze? Not a bit. The people? Not really. I just hope the ones that had problems found help and found themselves. Don't get me wrong, I don't think everyone who drinks has a problem. But for the ones that do have a problem, I hope they find a way to get to a place to face their lives, live their lives, learn to love themselves and not drink to cover their personal problems.

"Once I learned who I was, as screwed-up as I was, and learned to face my problems, many of which were the same as the problems everyone deals with everyday, life became easier. Sound weird? Recognize that you have problems and are flawed and you are better?"

"Seems to be working for you," Love responded.

"At least today," Tom replied harkening back to the old AA phrase "One Day at a Time."

He grew silent as he remembered what he had told

many acquaintances as they were either going into or considering going into, some form of drug treatment, "You are going to meet a lot of new people in your journey, the most important of which will be you. Be open to meeting the new you and you just might make a new friend."

Tom wondered if this advice had been as impactful to those receiving it, as he had hoped.

It certainly had worked for him.

Honesty, clarity, awareness, openness, and empathy — his lessons learned. Had he lost sight of these? Was he still facing his challenges or had something else replaced his old love of the drink?

* * *

Tom felt a sensation of ascending. At the same time he felt a gentle cooling and dampening in his environment. Love had returned him to where she had found him on the side of the hill.

The hill had not changed, but had Tom?

Love was now looking at Tom with an increasing level of understanding and empathy, falling short of total forgiveness and sympathy. She held the combined memories of women with whom Tom had spent time and been intimate, happy, disingenuous, engaged in a caring relationship, and spent just enough time to satisfy his sexual urges. Did she pity him? Not in the least, as he had control of his life and the choices he had made. But that was easy for Love to say and she knew it.

Back in the day, he was handsome, charming, intelligent, and in need of comfort. He had known it and leveraged it all to get what he wanted and needed. Love had accepted it all and made her choices to accept his advances and kindnesses. While there was a little pain in some of her memories, the joys far outweighed them. "We all got what we wanted and needed at the time," she thought to herself.

But it was clear that he was scarred and this presented itself periodically these many years later— perhaps less frequently, but just as assuredly as years before. This made Love want to mother Tom but her time with him was coming to an end. She assessed that he had come a long way toward understanding why he was where he was and that he was close to being able to answer the questions she hit him with when they first met.

Love was also beginning to feel all the emotions she had told herself she would never feel for Tom again. It wasn't so much passion as compassion. She could see the Tom that had been all potential and possibility. He still had time.

"What will become of our Tommy Boy?" she thought to herself.

But her turn and time with Tom was over.

"Tom? You okay, Honey?" she asked and really wanted to know. Not that she could do anything to address a negative response.

"I have no freaking idea!" he responded quickly. "You ever see the old TV show 'This is Your Life'?" he asked, realizing immediately that whatever Love was, she was probably not a big TV watcher, unless it was something that impacted his life in a big way. "It never seemed to be as emotional as what I just watched. But you covered most of the highlights or should I say low lights. And thanks for sparing the details of my inebriated activities. I was told I had a good time. I only have partial memory of that period—some positive and some negative. How did you phrase it? 'The good and the bad'?"

"Well, I do remember that we did have a good time together," Love agreed.

"Nice and I'm glad. And now I am with a great gal and have a great marriage. I'm doing very well, thank you," Tom said.

"Really?"

"Well… until tonight," Tom said.

* * *

CHAPTER III
PRESENT TENSE

He began to recognize his old haunts, the rainy and cold side of the hill. He found it hard to believe that it could be colder and darker than it was when he was here last—here at the site of the accident—but it was. His leg wasn't getting any better and he could now actually hear the pounding in his head. Whatever drug Love had given him had certainly worn off.

His focus returned to Love only to find that the light was making her image progressively more blurry. And her attention was no longer on him as she seemed to be looking toward something off in the distance.

Her image had now evolved into a silhouette against the dim light that slowly turned toward him. "Well Hi there, Tom," said the figure now in front of him. He certainly didn't know who or what this was, but it was clear that it wasn't the lovely Love.

"What happened to Love?" he called out.

"Well Goddamn, Tom, that is exactly what we are here to figure out! She told me that you were bright, but I didn't know that you had already figured out the key to all of this."

Tom was not sure if his shock was from the return of his pain and the renewed symptoms from what he now thought was at least a grade 2 concussion, or the abrupt departure of Love.

"What the hell are you talking about? Where's Love and who the hell are you?" he blurted out.

"OK. OK. So a couple of steps forward and a step back. Love told me that you are big on names but she didn't tell me you had arrived at the correct question. Very impressive Big Fella!"

"Again, what are you talking about?" he winced as the hot poker had returned to his knee.

"Where's Love, Buddy? Where's Love? With all respect to the Bard, 'That is the Question!' So we are on our way, Dude. Let me take a wild stab and see how far you really have come...do you know where Love is?"

"Give me an F-ing break. I asked you where she is and now I get it the same question back at me? Are you a shrink?"

"Oh. OK. Got it. You hit the right question by luck. Got the *what* but not the *why*. OK. We'll work on that."

"And who is we?"

"Oh sorry, I thought Love told you. You can call me Carin. It's easy for you to remember and it will have more meaning a little later."

"Are you another one of my hallucinations or did you stop on the road and see me down here?" Tom asked, knowing full well the answer but hoping upon hope that he was getting closer to being rescued.

"I really appreciate the walk or float through memory lane, I just wish that it got me closer to someone that can help me," he thought to himself.

"Oh I can and will help you, Big Fella!" Carin said out loud.

"What? How? I didn't say anything. How did you…" Tom started to ask.

"Well let's just say I've got skills," Carin interrupted. "Some of them come with age, and some are just from being very, very special. So it's up to you how you want to communicate. I can go either way. It's up to you, but realize that I hear EVERYTHING."

"Excuse me?!" her voice boomed. "Now we can do this nicely or not so nicely but the fact is that we ARE going to do this thing, whether you like it or not. And while I may not be as attractive as Love, trust me, my friend, I deserve better than what you just called me."

As if on cue, she moved into some reflected light and was revealed. It was clear that she had strength, confidence, and brains. She appeared older than Love, maybe early 40's. She was attractive, and dressed more conservatively than Love, in a loose fitting expensive-looking dark blue top and slacks. Her looks communicated that she had some significant life experiences and still maintained a simple beauty with a particular fire in her eye. Tom's immediate impression was that she was like one of his wife's soccer mom friends from the neighborhood. He would soon find out how wrong he was.

"I'm sorry. I was just..." Tom started to explain.

"Stop. Stop now! I don't give a crap what you were trying to do, Bubba. MY world is the one of reality: the here and now. No intentions. No meaning-to's. No trying. Only what you did, what you do, and the effect it has on others. I'm a bottom-line kind of girl. Sound familiar, Mr. Executive? And since I am not particularly pleased with your shitty little vocabulary, let's dispense with the small talk and move right to the task at hand, shall we?"

Tom just nodded, coming to the conclusion that once again his mind was going to take control of the situation and it had even gone to the trouble of including telepathy in the scenario. But did she have to be so controlling?

"You haven't seen controlling yet, Tommy Boy. By the way, I heard you like that name. So do I. So let's get going." With that she reached down, grabbed him under the arm, and effortlessly, though painfully for Tom, pulled him up to his feet.

"Oh, did I forget to mention the word "real"? No morphine-like touch from me. What you see, what you feel, what you cause, is what you get. Got it? So are you ready to go see the Fam now, Tommy?"

Despite his spinning head and the severe pain in every part of his body, Carin's reference to his family enabled him to muster up the energy to respond verbally with a loud, "Hell yeah. It's about Goddamn time! I thought you were just another visitor. But you actually can get me outta here? Get me home?"

"Oh yeah, we're going to your house alright, but just

like with Love, you will be a silent observer. I'm going to give you the opportunity to see and hear what most people would die for," she said. "You are going to see what people say and do when you're not around and particularly what they say and think about you."

Tom's dumbfounded look belied the fact that his mind was still working. A fact not lost on Carin "Very good, Tommy Boy," she chuckled. "You're right. This is not something most would literally die for – and you won't have to either. Relax, I am not here to help mark the end of Tommy. You still have some time left. By the way, how's that knee thing going, Big Fella? You know it wouldn't have hurt you to work out once in a while.

"What? Oh yes I do know how hard you 'F-ing' work. I also know the impact that it has had on you. But what we are going to experience right now doesn't involve what I know. It is all about you and what you know. And I won't be finished with you until I'm confident that your knowledge has risen to an acceptable level.

"I can tell you're still a little challenged on the vocabulary front," she continued. "I am going to give you a pass on that, even if your wife and your Mom never did. Oh yeah, I know about your Mom still correcting your grammar. But that's not the bigger issue is it? I bet you don't use that foul language when your Mommy's around now do you? So why me? You have 'respect for authority' issues? Or are you still just a Momma's boy?" she asked as she gave him a little kick in the knee.

"Ouch...shit!" he yelled. "Can we just get going? Not sure I can withstand any more of this painfully long introduction."

"Sure, here goes, "she said as her vice grip squeezed

his upper arm to the point well beyond any blood pressure monitor he had ever felt. "Oh buck up, you Wuss. And no, your biceps and triceps have not merged, although I can arrange it. And by the way, from here on out, the pain you're going to experience will most likely make you forget your little bumps and bruises—just something to look forward to, Tommy Boy."

While Love had had a more abrupt way of moving from one event from his past to another, Carin's approach was more gradual. With Carin, Tom seemed to experience a flowing sensation of movement.

The two of them quickly rose above his Man Cave and were above the clouds within a few seconds. While Tom felt some discomfort from the friction of the air on his body, the movement seemed to calm his major injuries. As the two of them broke back down through the clouds the descent slowed to eventually enable them to make a very gentle landing, a landing that included moving effortlessly through the solid roof and second floor of his home.

Yes, he was there at his home, but as with Love, he was an observer, not a participant.

There she was, his lovely wife Denise. He saw her moving around the kitchen and family room straightening various things. He thought about his mind's ramblings when the accident had first occurred. Was he just an observer and not a participant in his marriage?

"Damn right you are! And by the way, kudos to you, Big Guy. You are starting to ask some quality questions," Carin blurted out, reminding Tom of her unique talent of "hearing" his every thought. He was jolted by the familiar ring of his wife's cell phone.

"So does she," Carin commented in response to Tom's

fleeting thought of how great it would be if the call his wife was taking was from him.

> *"Hello?" she said without checking the display on her phone, subconsciously delaying the anticipated disappointment in learning that the caller was indeed not her husband.*
>
> *"Oh, it's you," she responded to her recognition of the caller's identity, namely her dear friend and neighbor, Pam Nolan. After a pause, she apologized to Pam for the tone of disappointment in her voice, "I'm sorry.... no....I'm glad you called. I was just thinking it might be Tom. I haven't heard from him tonight and with this crazy weather and the late hour, I'm getting a little worried. But I probably shouldn't worry. Lately 10 p.m. would be an early evening."*

Carin then demonstrated more of her mystical powers, as she seemed to flip a volume switch and Tom was now able to hear Pam as well.

> *"DD, you deserve better than this. Look what you have done for him...everything that you gave up and for what? Not this! Not that Brad and Jamie aren't great kids and a blessing. They are. But where the hell did Tom go?"*
>
> *"Pam, I think he's still there. It's just that when I retired it put a strain on the cash flow and he kicked his work ethic into high gear. As everything equalized after a couple of years and his income went up, he kept up the habit. And I also think his responsibilities from the last promotion just require a lot of time on the job. I guess it could be worse and he could be an irresponsible bum. He*

is certainly not that."

"Well he's not the same Tom he was!" Pam asserted, not wanting to let it go.

"Well Pamster, none of us are the same as we 'were'. I'm not an apologist for him but I do understand the pressure he felt when it became just him bringing in the cash. Not that I feel guilty about retiring because we discussed the whole lifestyle/child rearing/financial trilogy before I started staying home. We agreed that with the kids three and one, it was the right thing for all of us."

"DD, I agree, but does that mean that you signed his license to be an absentee father and husband? They could write a TV show about you and call it Bachelorette Mother!"

Pam was always coining little witty phrases, usually tied to TV, Tom thought.

"That was actually a pretty good one, Tommy," Carin interjected.

"Cute, Pam, cute. You do have a point about his not being around here very much. It seems like every week it's a new challenge and a new excuse. We have a soccer party for Brad's team this Friday. Tom promised Brad and me that he'd be there, but I doubt it. And if it was the first time he bagged out, that would be one thing. But it has become a pattern."

"Wrong, wrong, wrong."

"I know," Denise agreed. "When it started it was a disappointment to the kids and me when he missed an event. And then I noticed the jealousy. Brad started having issues with some of the kids whose dads were always around. Finally it turned into kind of a joke inside and

outside of the family. I guess it was just our way of dealing with it."

"You mentioned Brad's jealousy, what about yours?"

"She's not a shit disturber Tom, she's just calling a spade a spade," Carin responded to Tom's thought, as he was becoming agitated with the conversation.

"What do you mean? I feel sorry for Brad and Jamie, for that matter, a little bit for me. We are missing out on family fun. But mostly I feel sorry for Tom because I don't think he knows what he's missing."

"I meant don't you get a little jealous of the moms whose husbands are spending time with the family?"

*"I don't think I'm **jealous**; I just miss what we had because it was great…he was there and we always seemed to laugh. Well, I guess I am jealous of what was and a little bit of what is keeping him away."*

"Well since YOU brought it up, girlfriend, you say it's a what that's keeping him away – work — but are you sure it isn't a who?"

"Pam, I gotta tell ya, I almost wish it was another woman, cuz then I could compete. But I honestly don't think it is."

"Well good for you, Babe! Thanks for believing in me," Tom said aloud.

Carin proceeded to provide another painful squeeze, admonishing him, "Shhhh, Big Fella. Stick to learning mode. This is about her, not props for your fidelity."

"Well I don't know. He's awfully smart and men can be devious when covering things up"

"Pam," Denise interrupted, "let me say that you know I appreciate your friendship and views, but I am not going there. I'm more concerned about our life, my life, and the kids than any romantic drama."

"OK, OK, I'll stop. But you do have options."

"I know. And I have to admit that for the first time in our relationship I am starting to think about them," Denise said

"I'm really worried that even if he did start showing up to events and spending time with us, he wouldn't really be there. You know what I mean? Just because he's there, wouldn't mean he was really 'there.' I'm not saying that I'm sure about all this, but if it is going to be that way, I don't want to live in that kind of relationship."

"I'm so sorry Dee. I would imagine the doubt alone has got to be rough," Pam added in a supportive way.

"It is. And the kids deserve better. I mean what they see in us and our relationship is going to impact how they act as they get older. They just deserve better role models. In a way, it's their marriage too."

Tom's anger was morphing into sadness prompting Carin to remark, "Stay with us, Tommy Boy."

"And the worst thing about all of this is that I don't feel I can discuss it with Tom. The events and schedule, sure, but not my real feelings.

"I have actually started thinking about what I would need to do if we weren't together. Not the dating and relationship crap, but getting back into the rat race and resurrecting my career. I even placed calls to some of my old colleagues. After they got over the shock of hearing *my voice and then why I was calling, they painted a pretty good picture of opportunities for me. A lot has happened in the last 8 years, but I, and they, think I could get back into it and survive." Denise paused as she seemed to be summoning the strength to continue.*

"God Pam, am I really saying this? It's just so confusing and it hurts so much.

"I still love…," she started to break-up and couldn't speak anymore.

"You want me to come over?" Pam asked.

"No, thanks. I gotta go," Denise said as she completely lost it.

"This is not about you being misunderstood, Tom. This is all about her and the kids," Carin told Tom.

His jaw was locked open in amazement. As Carin looked at Tom's face, she was not sure if the tear coming from his eye was from the frustration he felt from his belief that Denise was mistaken, or the sadness at things having gotten this far and Denise's unhappiness.

* * *

As they stood there watching Denise crying, still holding the phone to her heart, Tom and Carin heard a ruckus from upstairs.

"No, you can't do anything to help her right now. Let's check-up on the rug rats upstairs," Carin said as she firmly gripped his elbow and led a wincing Tom up the stairway.

The two kids were engaged in a lively discussion in Jamie's room when Tom and Carin arrived.

"Does Mom know?" Jamie, Tom's precocious 9 year old daughter asked her older brother, Brad.

"Yep," Brad replied.

"Dad?" she continued.

"C'mon, when does he ever know anything?" asked Brad, not expecting an answer.

"They do talk sometimes, you know."

"When? In their sleep?"

"Well he's going to be pissed off when he does find out," Jamie warned.

"Since when do you say 'pissed'?" While Brad was only 12, he viewed himself as the 'much' older brother and with a parental tone, he was expressing that he was in no hurry to see his little sister grow up.

"I am 10!" Jamie proclaimed.

"9," Brad corrected.

"Going on 10!"

"Whatever. It's just summer soccer league. Besides when was the last time you saw him at one of my soccer games? Like never. When was the last time he went to ANY of our stuff?"

"That's not fair," Jamie protested, revealing her

belief in Denise's 'company line'. "He has a real important job that makes him work a lot. Mom sez he has to do it to pay for all of our stuff. He always asks about our sports when he is here."

"You're right, but I still don't think he cares that much about it anymore."

"Oh yeah? Then why don't you tell him? Cuz you know he's gonna get mad."

"I didn't say he wouldn't get pissed off and yell and everything. He'll be hecka pissed. But I still don't think he really cares. He just has his list of things that we're supposed to do and he gets mad when we don't do them. I don't think he cares about the soccer team. I think he would just be annoyed that I'm not following his list."

"You should still tell him," Jamie shared, not wanting to let it go. "He'll be hecka MORE mad if you wait and he finds out. What do think he will do if he gets home early one day and wants to go to one of your games? Or someone says something at that soccer party on Friday?"

"C'mon James. That's not going to happen. Besides Mom said it was ok that I quit. I've wanted to join Band for a long time and now I'm going to do it."

"Brad is a band geek! Brad is a band geek! Band Geek! Band Geek!"

PUNCH. Brad had a short fuse for being taunted, particularly from this little girl, and decided to put an end to it. The knuckle punch hit its mark on Jamie's shoulder.

"Better to be a band geek than to waste my time kicking a ball around. Gawd, I hate soccer."

"I'm gonna tell mom you said God!"

After a second punch, Brad replied with a warning tone, "No you won't.

"You remember last year on Thanksgiving when Dad gave that long speech at dinner. He was all 'you should be thankful for this and very thankful for that', (with a poor attempt to imitate his father's voice) and then he went on with 'because you have been given all this stuff, you have to participate in all this other stuff.' Blah blah blah. He went on forever."

Tom was shocked at what he considered to be a complete misinterpretation of what he thought was an outstanding piece of parental advice. As he silently criticized his son's perspective, Carin delivered a formidable knuckle punch of her own to his shoulder. "His belief is his reality, Tommy Boy. Listen up."

"He did not!" Jamie protested.

"Did too."

"Did not. He just repeated it so he would be sure that YOU heard him."

"Well it seemed like forever. Anyway he was all 'you need to be rounded' and everything."

"Well-rounded," Jamie corrected.

"Whatever. He wanted us to do shit, because 'the more you do, the more you do' and 'idle hands are the devil's workshop.' He's giving us these dumb sayings but what about thinking about what I WANT to do?"

"Mooom, Brad is swearing again! He said the S word."

Boom. Brad delivered another punch. "Brad that one hurt. You don't have to hit me that hard. Mom can't ever hear up here."

> "K. Anyway, I'm gonna drum and that's it."
>
> "OK, but he's still gonna find out. He'll hear you practice and you are gonna get in trouble. He'll ask you at dinner, 'Howz it goin' with soccer?' Ya know when he runs out of people to talk about with Mom and he asks about our stuff? That's when you're gonna get nailed. Brad's gonna get it! Brad's gonna get it!"
>
> "Well I'm gonna ride it out as long as I can. By the time he finds out it will be too late and I can use all that commitment stuff he always talks about."

Tom's anger shifted to a sense of sadness as he observed what he considered to be a failure in his ability to effectively impart his values to his son. A little pinch from Carin brought him back into what was transpiring in Jamie's room.

> "Besides, Mom says he's too busy right now and we shouldn't get him pissed. Like telling him about your Math grade. Jamie's gonna get it!" Brad proclaimed in an excellent version of his sister's voice. "Jamie's gonna get it!"
>
> "But you and Mom forgot one very important thing smarty pants," Jamie said confidently. "Dad loves sports. He talks about it all the time. He even golfs! And how is he going to show off to Kerry and Kim's Dad and Mr. Gould? He always tells them how good you are. He even talks about my gymnastics to them. And what about Papa and Mamage? What's he going to tell them about? Huh? He even tried to make us swimmers, like him! If you aren't a jock you aren't cool—It's the Daniels Family tradition. It's what keeps you from being a girly girl!" Jamie breaks out into uncontrollable laughter.

For a brief moment, Brad is speechless.

Tom was shocked and getting sadder by the minute. "Yes Big Fella, that IS what they really think. For all the right reasons you may have been wanting to expose them to all that you gained from your childhood athletic experiences. But sometimes that acorn tumbles a distance away from the oak. They are their own people, not you."

Brad responds to his sister's logic by jumping on her and covering her head with a pillow. " And I'm gonna keep you from becoming a Girly Girl." After a moment he lifts the pillow from her head, but stays on top of her. "I'm gonna be a good drummer. Be in a rock band. What if he just told them all what I'm doing and said I was really good at it? Huh? Isn't that the point? To be good and have fun doing it?"

"Yeah right. You in a rock band!!!"Uncontrollable laughter returned as she nodded her head to a song going through her head.

"You are so weird!" Brad declared as he returned the pillow to Jamie's face.

Both of his children were laughing.
Tom was not.

*   *   *

Carin wasn't in the mood to let Tom wallow in the disappointment he felt from observing the conversations involving Denise and his kids. And she chose to not impart any further verbal abuse, sensing that she had successfully secured his attention and he had a lot to think over. But that didn't stop her from giving him a quick, sharp slap on the backside so he would be aware of the significant change in venue.

After absorbing the blow it took him a moment to realize where he was. Once he did, his reaction was immediate. "Well alrighty, then. Now we're talkin'. If you were going to take me anywhere to recover, you couldn't have picked a better spot," Tom happily exclaimed.

"I'm so glad you're pleased, Tommy Boy," she responded with not a small dose of sarcasm. "But I think you understand that your pleasure has nothing to do with my motivation. If you feel comfort in being here with your golfing buddies, I am glad for you."

"You bet. We live for the Saturday game. There's a group of about 10 of us that get together every Saturday at our club, Hillwood Country Club. A round of golf on Saturday morning is the perfect way to start a weekend. And as much as we have The Game in common as a bond, a trust, and a camaraderie that is just great, we are a rather eclectic group."

"Well good for you. Sounds a little excessive on the Man-love front, but as enthusiastic as you are, I hope you enjoy your visit to the links today.

"How many are we today?" Tommy G. asked Ron as he burst into the clubs members' grille that doubled as the pre-round gathering spot. Ron was filling out the

pairings for the game while some of the others —Chris, Mike, Johnny, Marv, Andy, and Mark — were wolfing down a pre-game breakfast.

"Only 8 today," Ron responded.

"Don't see Tom yet. He coming?" Tommy G. asked.

"I didn't hear from him, so I assume not."

"What's with that?"

"I think he's just slammed at work. You know as well as anyone what that place can do to you," chimed in Mike. Tommy G. had retired from Tom's company a few years earlier and both Ron and Mike had each worked there for a decade prior to leaving.

"Yeah, but he used to be the one who was always here first in the morning and never missed a week. Don't get it," Tommy G. responded.

"Maybe he's trying to keep up with you, G., by burning himself out. He is pretty competitive"Chris threw out trying to get a rise out of Tommy G. with a little dig.

"Tommy's right though. Tom used to live for the Saturday game. I don't know what's going on, but it can't be good," Andy observed.

"We all know what that place is like, but not on Saturday mornings," Tommy G. protested.

"Maybe he's already burnt," Mark interjected.

"No they don't sound like a bunch of women, Tommy Boy. And I am warning you that your sexism quotient is on the rise. Maybe they just care," Carin said in response to Tom's unspoken criticism of the group.

"Maybe Denise has got him tied up with the honey-do list," Johnny suggested.

"I doubt it. He doesn't have a home maintenance

bone in his body. Outside of his gardening, the only tool he knows how to use is his debit card. But since you brought her up, Judy said that she had a chat with Denise last week and things are not all roses at the Daniels house," Mike threw out.

"Guys this is none of our business," Marv admonished, feeling that the Boys had crossed the line.

"You're right Marv, but no shit Mike?" Tommy G. said." I always thought they seemed pretty tight and Tom's always talking about how good a thing they have."

"Has anyone talked to him lately? Should we check-in with him?" Chris asked.

"Guys, this is none of our Goddamn business," Marv repeated, having already heard far more than he wanted and felt anyone needed.

"You're right. It's his gig. He'll sort it out. I don't think he's going to want us getting into his shit," Tommy G. informed the table as though it was his idea.

"Yeah, but at least we could get him out here for a couple of weeks. His handicap had gotten pretty low before he stopped playing. If we could get him back out at least we could get some money off of him until his game gets back in shape," Ron suggested.

"Great point," Mark agreed. "Who's got his cell number?" he asked to laughter from everyone at the table.

"Oh, I don't think they have given up on you quite yet. Sounds like they still care," Carin shared.

"I know I've been missing a few games, but it's a pretty big leap for them to think I have such big issues," Tom said.

"Maybe they know you, or at least the signs, better than you do."

As he listened to the banter amongst his buddies, in addition to being relieved that he did not linger as the object of the conversation, Tom realized how much he missed his time on the course with the Boys.

Denise had convinced him to join the Club so that, as she put it, " For at least 4 hours a week you'll be able to get out, relax, have some fun, and get some exercise."

"Pretty sound reasoning, Big Fella. I wonder how many guys are 'forced' to join a golf club because of their wife's care for their well-being?" Carin shared without being asked.

In terms of the reasoning and Denise's uniqueness, there was no debate, Tom thought. He really had withdrawn—or at least just stopped prioritizing — this part of his life. Tom couldn't figure out if it was a conscious decision or if he was just lazy. If it was the former, he couldn't remember doing so. If it was the latter, it just seemed to be consistent with the attention he was paying to the rest of his relationships.

And now Denise was talking to her friends about it.

"She has to talk to someone, Tommy. And it doesn't appear that you have been very available lately," Carin shared.

Tom's head started spinning, connecting this aspect of his life to the rest of what Carin had showed him. Had he made conscious decisions that led him to a pattern of isolation, or at a minimum, disengagement with everyone in his life? Or had he just become *lazy* with that as well?

Whatever it was, it was clear that it wasn't good.

The bigger question in his mind was whether he could

regain the balance and focus, if he could "get out, relax, have some fun, and get some exercise," across the board.

"Now we're getting somewhere, Mr. Daniels," Carin thought to herself.

*   *   *

CHAPTER IV
POSSIBILITIES

Tom closed his eyes and let out a huge sigh.

"What have I done? How did they get so disconnected? How did *I* get so disconnected?" he thought considering everyone he had just visited.

As he awaited some kind of response from Carin, he was surprised that his questions were met with silence.

He opened his eyes expecting to see Carin, but was shocked to find that he was back on the hill in his cave with a new woman standing before him.

Tom had been around thousands of businesswomen

in his career and recognized the look—the serious one. It conveyed a single-mindedness and lack of respect for the need of social graces or niceties that could rival any man's. If it wasn't necessary to get to the intended result, it was useless. As much progress had been made in the business world relative to gender equality, these qualities were still noticed more when possessed by a woman, and rarely in a positive way.

Her hair was dark and pulled back tightly behind her head, held there by an extensive configuration of clips and pins. Her glasses had a stylish frame that sent a message of seriousness and severity, as they were a little heavier than they needed to be. That she had glasses at all said that the woman had not had surgery to correct her vision nor chosen to wear contacts. If she was wearing make-up, he could not see it. Apparently vanity was not a trait that Tom had in common with her.

Tom sensed that the dark business suit she wore was replicated in various colors at least 10 times in her closet, if women/spirits like these actually had wardrobes.

There was a conservatism to her appearance that differed from the normal hi-tech executive look for women, even on their most formal days. If the suit had been black, he would have guessed her profession to be that of a mortician, a thought that sent a painful shiver through his still pain-stricken body and made him again think of Dickens' *A Christmas Carol*, this time of its third, post-death spirit.

"Holy shit! A black suit! Is this what this has all come to?" he let slip out.

"No. But what I am about to share with you, the future, your future, may be worse than what I am guessing you think I represent," she said in a very straightforward, calm, and lawyer-like manner.

"What could be worse than death?" he asked.

"My girls tell me you were learning. That is an excellent question and one that only you can answer."

"You guys are sure long on questions but pretty short on answers," Tom proclaimed. "And by the way, what is your name again?"

"Well you can call me Liv. And the answers you seek are there for the taking, but as Love and Carin shared with you, that is up to you. After my brief visit you will have all that you need."

"What I need is to have somebody find me and get me out of here," Tom reiterated.

"We are providing you with what you need 'to get out of here', but again, how you handle things from there is entirely up to you. If you are ready, can we proceed?"

"Sure. Go ahead. Beat me up while I'm down. Let's get it over with," Tom said, looking for some sympathy even though he knew it would not be forthcoming.

With that, Tom and Liv were instantly at his house, standing in the front yard. The perfectly manicured lawn and garden were cluttered with various boxes, pieces of furniture, and equipment associated with the very large moving van in the driveway.

Then Tom saw Denise.

Denise was standing in the driveway, drinking a Starbuck's latte when Pam approached.

> *"How ya doin'?" Pam inquired with the conversation opener Denise had been hearing for the last decade.*
> *As Denise attempted to respond, all the emotions she*

had tried to suppress over the last couple of years bubbled to the top and she could only produce an "I don't know" shrug. She began to weep, glad that the kids weren't home and couldn't see her.

"So the day is finally here," she struggled to share. "The day I never wanted to come. Ever since the divorce forced us to sell the house, I just wanted this day to be over."

"I know how tough it has been for you, but other than right this second, how are you holding up?" Pam asked.

"Except for the logistics of closing on my new condo, and making sure these movers get our stuff over there, I'm not sure about anything."

"How long were you here, D, 12 years?"

"10, but it's not just the move or even all of the real estate crap," she paused, gathering herself to continue. "It's EVERYTHING. All of the tactical stuff since we separated was a challenge. But to take care of all that, I just blocked out all the emotions...until today. Pam, this really hurts!"

"I know, I know," Pam said as she stepped forward and hugged Denise close. Pam felt her friend go limp and then sob into her shoulder.

After a few silent moments, Denise pulled back, apologized, and explained, "I knew this was going to be hard, but I didn't realize how much there was to do and how lonely I would feel doing it."

"That asshole!" hissed Pam.

"I don't think that we...." Denise started.

"Don't you go defending him. He is the reason that today is happening. He is the reason you and the kids are being up-rooted. He is the reason you hurt."

"Well let's just say that things didn't work out the way we'd planned. But on the bright side, I am getting back into the swing of things at work. With all the new office tools, and things online, everything sure move at a faster pace than it used to. The fundamentals of the business are pretty much the same, but the way things get done has really changed. But I'm catching up.

"People have been really great. It seems that I am not the only one that has gone through this divorce crap. The number of people that have either been divorced or are on their way to it, is astounding. And there is this one guy there…"

"Oh my God! DD Daniels! You mean you are doing more at work than work? Tell me EVERYTHING."

"Let's not get ahead of ourselves. We went out for drinks and he seems really nice. But we are taking things very slowly and I am not talking about it to many people, particularly not the kids. We aren't a couple or anything."

"OK, but how exciting is that?! Speaking of the kids, how are they doing with everything?" Pam asked.

"Well that's pretty complicated. Jamie's handling things better than Brad is. But you know how she is; she's more emotionally mature in a lot of ways than Brad.

"Her gymnastics keeps her focused and the discipline from that is also helping her at school. And then there's the relationship that every little girl has with her Daddy," Denise's voice started to break up again when she said Daddy. "She really looks forward to the weekends that she spends with Tom."

"Well that's good," observed Pam.

"Brad, on the other hand, is not handling things well at all. It's gotten so bad that I try not to answer the phone for fear that it's another call from the school. He's angry and won't see a counselor. I know he's mad – and sad – about the divorce but I'm beginning to worry that he's clinically depressed.

"And then there's the new friends he's hanging out with. I hate to be superficial but the way they look...I don't know...it's negative and antagonistic. And they're sullen and disrespectful around me. This is so not Brad. I worry about how they're influencing him. He's vulnerable right now, no matter how tough he tries to act. He's incredibly sensitive and very susceptible to being sucked into this group in a deeper way.

"I just hope we haven't lost him," Denise said between renewed sobs.

"And Tom?" Pam asked, after Denise waved away another hug.

"That's another issue. The weird thing is that the only time Brad seems to open up to me is when he talks about dreading going over to his father's. It's as though he hates him.

"While Tom and I may not be together anymore, Brad still needs a father.

"I mentioned the school calling? Brad's grades are just horrible and those friends I mentioned are part of this band they've formed. And let's just say these kids are not on the Honor Roll.

"I hope moving into the new house will help. I pray Brad doesn't start getting into drinking or drugs. With Tom's history, that's something we've always been worried about," Denise exhaled and seemed calmer, as

though getting all these worries out had helped.

"Where is Tom in all this?" Pam asked, trying to stifle her anger with him.

"You know, it may surprise you, but he's actually been as supportive as I could have hoped for. I mean it's still awkward between us in terms of our relationship. I think he still doesn't get it from that side of things. But with all of the practical matters and things we have to interact on, he's been fine."

"I meant with the Brad and Jamie stuff?" Pam clarified, flirting with prying.

"Oh that. On that front he's been great. You know I think he is more engaged with the kids now than when we were together. As I mentioned, he and Jamie are totally cool. He shows up at their events and even went to Jamie's Parent-Teacher conference last week.

"But the Brad thing is a tough one. I don't know that it's Tom's fault, but I do know that he is really struggling with it. I think that sometimes his efforts to make things right with Brad are making things worse. It's just really hard for all of us."

Tom was stunned. He couldn't understand how things could ever progress to this point. Any positives that could be drawn from Denise and him apparently making the best out of bad situation were completely overshadowed by his fears around the negative direction that his son's life had taken.

His biggest fear as a father had always been that his children's genetic predisposition to follow in their father's drug-induced footsteps would be realized.

He was quiet and crushed. He turned away and looked

up to the sky.

* * *

As Tom looked back to the scene in front of his house, he was startled by an abrupt change in location. He was no longer in front of his "former" home.

"We've moved forward a bit. This is the new townhouse where the former Mrs. Daniels lives with her two children," Liv shared in response to the confused look on Tom's face.

Tom then observed an all-too-quickly maturing young lady running out to meet a slightly older version of himself, at his car. Who was this young lady getting into the car?

> "Hi Jamester," Tom greeted his daughter as she piled her gymnastics paraphernalia into the backseat, now getting a little crowded with Carin and the younger Tom in tow.
>
> "Hi Tomster," answered Jamie, now a maturing 12 year old with more than her share of sass.
>
> "Hi who?"
>
> "Tomster. You don't like that name? Well guess what? Jamester doesn't work either."
>
> "OK, J. You got it. You all set? Gonna dazzle them today?"
>
> "Think so. I have everything down except my new routine on the beam," she said, referring to the Balance Beam, the event in the all-around competition that challenged her the most. "My coach said I had to add some more difficulty and she definitely did that. I've been

practicing it. I'll be OK, if I can just nail the dismount."

"I'm sure you'll be great. How's everything else? School?" Tom asked as they pulled away from the new townhouse.

"School's good, but I don't understand why I have to take Spanish. I'm planning on living in America all my life so it seems pretty stupid to have to learn a different language. But everything else is OK."

"Your Mom OK?" Tom asked as though he had not even heard his daughter's response to his first question. An oversight that Jamie did not miss.

"Dad, don't start this. Ask her."

"Alright, just checking in on how you guys are doing with all of the changes."

"Changes?" she asked. "Is that code for the dreaded D-word—DIVORCE?"

"Hey, you don't have to be that way. I just want to make sure you're OK. I am still your Dad, ya know."

"Duh! I know, but you're always bringing it up like it is a thing, like, 'How's the dog?' It's just the way it is."

"Well you know we still have arrangements with someone you can talk to about it if you want to. You know, if there's some things that are bugging you that you don't feel comfortable talking to me or your Mom about," Tom shared, trying to sell the concept softly but hoping that she would take him up on the offer.

"I know. You guys have been talking about this for a long time. Don't need it. And besides, why would I want to talk to a stranger about my personal stuff?" she asked.

"I kind of see them as professional friends that you can talk through problems with," Tom explained.

"Well I don't need to pay for friends. I am a VERY

popular girl!" Jamie laughed.

"I'm sure. But just so you know. It's there if you need it," Tom pressed, throwing out his last attempt at closing her on the concept.

"OK Dad. I know and I don't need it. You guys can relax. I'm not gonna go postal or anything. Sometimes people just fall out of love and when that happens, they get divorced. That's what happened to you and Mom. I wasn't real happy about it but I'm fine now."

Tom was floored and the shocked look on his face showed it.

His 30 year old, 12 year old continued, "I've got some friends whose parents don't get along and believe me, it's a lot worse than what I have to deal with!"

Passenger Tom's reaction matched that of his older driver. How the hell could a little girl get so wise?

"OK. Message received," Tom responded, appearing to bite his tongue. But it was clear there was nothing more to be gained by pressing the issue today.

"Remember, we need to park in the back. It's a lot closer to the participants' entrance," she reminded Tom.

"Got it. How's Brad?"

"Daaaaad! Just stop OK? You know he's weird. He talks to me about as much as he talks to you," she answered, not hiding her irritation.

"Just keep hoping you have some deets on what is going on with him."

"Nope. Can we just not talk about it? It makes me feel weird. You know how there are some things that you just don't like to discuss? Like when I tell you about Marcus?" she stated, referencing this month's boyfriend.

> "Who is Marcus?" Tom asked, feeling inadequate with his inability to keep up with Jamie's social life.
>
> "Who is Marcus?! He's my boyfriend! We've been going out for almost a whole month now!" she proudly stated. "He might even be there today. You want to meet him?"
>
> "Sure, that would be great," Tom responded, trying to hide his total lack of interest.

Tom was shocked on many levels. How could his daughter have such a mature attitude toward divorce? It had to have been a pretty traumatic event for her.

While she appeared to have adjusted to the new arrangement, he wondered if the conversation he had just observed was really revealing her acceptance of the current state of affairs, or something else. Was she instinctively adopting her father's approach to dealing with unhappiness? How far had the acorn fallen from the oak? He hoped with all of his heart that she had reconciled the split of her parents and wasn't a time bomb with a ticking fuse.

What he really thought was: how the hell do I get out of Liv's version of my future and get to the business of avoiding this situation completely?

* * *

"You asked about Brad so let's check in on him," Liv suggested. They moved instantly from the back seat of the car to the small office of Mr. Marshall, the Head Counselor at Brad's high school. The office seemed especially small due to the number of people crowded into it: Tom, Denise, Brad, and of course, Mr. Marshall.

Pleasantries were dispensed with very quickly as the reason for the meeting was understood prior to anyone's arrival.

"Brad, would you like to tell your parents why we're here—what happened today?" Mr. Marshall asked.

"No," he responded. "Everyone knows."

"OK. Well, let me just review what happened so we are all on the same page. Early this afternoon one of our security guards found Brad and two other boys out in the far corner of the parking lot drinking alcohol. I can't speak to whether they were drunk as we chose not to engage the authorities. If we had, they all would have received, at a minimum, a citation. Given that this is the first instance of Brad's engagement in this kind of activity, we chose to keep it at our level.

"What will be happening is that Brad will be suspended for a week and will be required to complete a 6 week drug and alcohol aversion program. He will need to be accompanied by one of you at each one of those sessions.

"Brad, is there anything else you want to share?"

"No. You guys are going to do what you are going to do. It's not like I have any say in what is going to happen here," Brad mumbled.

"Ok, please wait outside, I would like to speak to

your parents without you in the room."

After Brad left, Tom and Denise were provided with a more detailed review of Brad's situation delivered by the counselor. The grades, the friendships, and the attitude were all consistent. While not a surprise to the parents, it was still a depressing picture when viewed in the aggregate.

"Brad mentioned that the two of you are no longer together. I can assure you that I do not want to dive into that with the two of you, except to say that what I am seeing in Brad is consistent with similar scenarios…and with increasing frequency."

"What scenario are you referring to?" Denise asked.

"I'm sorry. I was referring to the reaction to a change in the family dynamic demonstrating itself in a negative change in the child's behavior."

"OK. Well as much as we have tried, we have been unsuccessful in getting him engaged with counseling," Denise said.

'The drinking is particularly concerning," Tom stated looking at Denise. After a thoughtful pause, "Mr. Marshall, to be completely candid, I have been sober for over 20 years and we have always been very open with the kids about the potential of their genetic predisposition toward addiction. While I don't want to over-react, I am concerned about whether this is just a one-time thing or there are other things happening, or about to happen, that are even more serious," Tom confided.

"I understand. It is not an easy situation,' Marshall observed.

"Another thing that I am worried about is that if we act firmly we may run the risk of pushing him even

further away...the old physics lesson: for every action there is an equal and opposite reaction. But we just can't look the other way, either," Tom said.

"Tom, we have some work to do." Denise said.

"Well you two, let us know if there is anything you need from us," Marshall said.

After Tom and Liv watched everyone exit the office, Tom was left dazed and confused. He closed his eyes and thought about how this was similar to some of the most challenging business situation he had dealt with in his career, situations in which there were many variables and questions. But unlike those business situations, he didn't have staff he could call on to fill in the data gaps required for him to make an intelligent decision about what he should do.

Was all of this happening simply because of the possible future split between him and Denise?

Was it down to Brad having to deal with two households and two sets of rules?

Was all of this just natural male adolescent rebellion against the rules?

Or was the primary cause associated with Tom's personal genetics, personality flaws, and addiction history?

"Pick your poison, Mr. Daniels," Tom said to himself. A, B, C, D, or all or some of the above. He felt uncertain of the answers and certainly ill-prepared to deal with any of them.

No matter what happened in his real future, he thought, he needed to do his best to either eliminate what he could, or at the very least, mitigate those factors which were not completely under his control.

★   ★   ★

Tom was now inside of a restaurant.

"Man, I wish you would give me a little warning on that location change," Tom requested.

"Why is that? There's nothing you can do at this moment to influence the version of your future I am presenting to you," Liv informed him in the pragmatic way that Tom was quickly tiring of.

"Fine...fine...But wait a sec. This isn't a future event. I recognize the restaurant. And look at that young girl at the table. I think you and Love got your lines crossed. This looks more like the past than the future.

"Look, that's Denise and me." Tom was immediately moved to a position behind the girl he referenced at the table and while it was true that the male figure sitting across the table from the girl/woman was Tom, it was not Tom in his 30's as he thought from his first impression.

Liv simply said, "I think her name is Tina and I guarantee that there is only one 20- or 30-something at that table."

"Holy Shit!" Tom said under his breath. He walked around the table under his own limited power to see Tina. She could have been Denise's sister. The hair was a little lighter, the eyes just a little more done-up, but that was definitely her...or her reincarnate.

He quickly moved back to his spot behind Tina to take a look at *himself*. Yes, he was older but something was different and he had to take a close look in the dim light of the restaurant. He seemed older but not, at the same time.

"How far into the future is this?" he asked Liv. Like every other time he posed a question to her, he received an 'I dunno' shrug. It was a bonus when she actually answered. Or was it?

Since he was on his own, he leaned in, sticking his face in over Tina's shoulder to get a closer look. The perfume from Tina was not cheap but far more pungent than anything that Denise had ever used.

"Oh My God!" He shouted, knowing by now that no one except he and Liv could hear him, even if she seemed thoroughly disinterested to most of what he said. "I'm dying!"

At that point Liv had to respond, "You're definitely aging but 'dying' might be a slight exaggeration."

"Not dying....but dyeing, as in dyeing my hair!"

With Tom's reaction to his discovery, even Liv had to crack a little smile. But then, "And my skin!!" sent her over the edge and she let out an uncharacteristic giggle, that she tried unsuccessfully to muffle with her hand.

Indeed, in an effort to recapture the Tom of an earlier day, the 47-year old version of Tom was now into cosmetics, heavily into cosmetics. And it was clearly not just the moisturizers that many men were now using to reduce the number and depth of their ever-increasing wrinkles. He was doing something to adjust his skin color.

His hair appeared almost completely void of any grey. While there were variations in the natural brown of his hair, there was none of the grey that had been creeping in since his late 20's.

As his artificial hair color was obvious to the younger Tom, someone less familiar with his natural appearance would not have picked-up on the artwork. However his "tan" was another story. To have skin that color was just not right. The only way one could characterize it was "fake". The late George Hamilton or any of the

Housewives reality show stars had nothing on him.

As the older version of Tom was trying to regain his youthful appearance, the current Tom was struck by the juxtaposition of the young woman/girl and the much older man. All his efforts to regain his youthful appearance had accomplished was to highlight the difference in their ages, a fact apparently completely lost on the aging man.

"All of this and she hasn't even opened her mouth yet," Tom thought. "Is this a sitcom? I can't wait to hear the intellectual discourse these two are going to have."

As Tom continued to watch this "odd couple", he noticed that they were quietly and gently caressing each other's hands while gazing into each other's eyes. The old valley-girl phrase 'gag me with a spoon' never had a better application. He wondered if the lack of conversation was due to the apparent enjoyment they were deriving from the 'lovey-dovey' activity, or from the fact that they didn't really have anything to say to one another.

He also concluded that if the two of them were just sitting at the table, sans public display of affection, most observers would assume Daddy was taking his daughter, his Little Girl, out for dinner.

Tom and even the disturbingly even-keel Liv, were both starting to get bored with the show when Tina provided insight into the nature of the relationship on view by breaking the romantic silence.

> "Oh Tommy, you are so sweet to me," she gushed. "This is just a wonderful place. How did you hear about it?"
>
> "One of the guys at work told me about it," he said,

"Well as long as I am with you, we could be anywhere," she breathed.

Tom was immediately concerned that between this desperately disgusting display and the normal effects of a concussion, he might very well vomit at any moment. He fought valiantly to overcome the urge.

"That's sweet, Tina," Tom said, appearing to make an effort to match her affection, but failing. His failure was lost on young Tina.

"I understand about this weekend, but I was really hoping to spend some more snuggle time."

Her speech was not directly out of the Valley Girl dialog catalog, but Tom thought of a variant of the old adage, saying to himself, "you can take the girl out of the Valley, but you can't take the Valley out of the girl."

"Are you sure that I can't come over, just for a little while?"

"Tina we discussed this, "Tom said as he withdrew his hands from the clutches of Tina's perfectly manicured hands. "They just aren't ready. And neither am I."

"I'll respect your wishes, but I still don't completely understand. I mean you've been separated for 18 months and divorced for almost a year. Don't you think that your kids think that you might be seeing someone?"

"Well, first of all, I don't think my kids think of me in terms of being a person that is or is not 'seeing someone'. Second, you are just going to have to trust me on this. When the time is right, I'll introduce you to Brad and Jamie. And if they do think that I am seeing

somebody, I just don't want to throw it in their face."

"Well at least I haven't lost it completely," Tom thought.

"But Tommy, they're teenagers. They'll be cool. And I know we'd get along. I still remember what it was like to be a teenager," she explained.

"Like it was yesterday? Because it was!" Tom observed, as a slight, sheepish grin arose from the stoic Liv.

"I really don't want to discuss this again," Tom stated firmly. He seemed to have a short fuse on this issue and it was approaching its end. "I told you when we first got together that it's complicated. It involves the kids, their mother, and my ability to continue to be involved with their parenting."

"What? Do you have an agreement with her that if you date anyone, you can't see the kids?" Tina protested. "I just sometimes think, ya know, that I embarrass you. You say you love me and how pretty I am. If I go to the gym any more than I do, they are going to start charging me rent in addition to the club fee you pay for! If I'm good enough for you, why aren't I good enough for them?"

"It has nothing to do with your appearance or our relationship. It's just too early."

Tina just wouldn't let go, "I think they've figured out that your marriage is over and the two of you are not getting back together. I mean, ya know, that is the case, right? I just want to be part of your life and I feel like I'm a second class citizen having to hide in the closet every time they come to stay with you for a weekend."

Before Tom blew up and shut Tina down, he remembered the discussions he had had with Denise about this very scenario, as they finalized the arrangements of their divorce.

He also appeared to have heard all of this many times before and was not enjoying himself. "Listen, that's it," Daddy told his Little Girl. "Tina, I do care for you and you are beautiful," he assured her in a softening tone. "Just give me this thing with the kids for a little while longer."

Based on Tina's reaction, she was pleased with the affirmation. And her apparent satisfaction at having registered her complaint, again, seemed to rise to a level of resolution in her mind. "I'll give you that if you promise to give me THAT thing after dinner," she said while reaching her hand under the small table's tablecloth to just the proper spot between his legs.

"OK, let's talk about the holiday weekend," she suggested with a little hop in her chair that seemed to signal an abrupt segue to a new, more positive subject. "My parents can't wait to meet you!"

"My God, do we really need to sit through this drivel?" Tom asked Liv.

"This drivel, as you call it, is a very likely eventuality. Are you suggesting that your vanity and lust for an attractive young woman are impossibilities?"

"I say that I have no interest in any other women and if I did, they wouldn't be closer to my children's age than mine! I've seen this scenario before. Marty Field dated a woman, more a girl, half his age after he divorced. There was something almost perverse about it. At first he thought it was so great parading around with his cute little trophy. And she seemed to genuinely care for him. I have to say we joked that her eyesight must have been worse than his.

"When his loins finally calmed downed, or ceased to function, Marty ended it. He told me that it was great 'in the moment', but they could never really connect past the initial excitement. We would have given him a much harder time about it, but I think he was really hurt and embarrassed when it didn't work out.

"I would never repeat his mistake."

"Really?" Liv questioned.

"I thought I told you that I would think about it and now you've gone and confirmed the date with your parents? And now it's a whole weekend in So Cal?! Let me check and I will let you know tomorrow."

Tina appeared surprised, "OK, I can kinda understand the deal with the kids, but what's the issue with my parents? They just want to meet this wonderful man I have fallen in love with!"

"I'm sorry, you're right. To be honest, it's been a long time since I had a Meet the Parents moment. I guess I'm okay with heading down there. I just need to psych up a little for it."

"I understand Tommy. But you can relax. I know you guys are really going to hit off," Tina reassured him.

"OK Babe, but let's make sure we are in sync. I'm just meeting them. I don't want us to be getting ahead of ourselves," he said.

"Don't worry, we're good. Speaking of how we're good, can we kind of hurry through dinner and head

home?" Tina asked making another reach under the table.

"Damn right you're getting ahead of yourself, Old Man!" Tom shouted.

"How long has it been? A year? And he is already talking 'love' and meeting the parents. And howz that gonna work? He is probably older than Mom and Dad. Now I'm getting interested. Can we come back and see how absurdly this plays out?" Tom asked.

"As awkward as the meeting might appear, it is something for which YOU set the stage. Do you really think you can go through all of the pleasant dating and 'falling in love' preliminaries and not be expected to follow through? I thought Carin was more effective than this."

★   ★   ★

"I hadn't originally planned on taking you here, but it appears there may be more value to it than I thought. Just know that your level of interest had absolutely no influence on my motivation," the ever personable Liv shared.

And with that Tom once again was struck with the pain of an immediate change in lighting. This time he found himself and his companion viewing the 47 year old version of himself in the backyard of a very large house, or more appropriately characterized as a mansion. Given Liv's intro, it was clear that he was at Tina's parents' home. And a large one it was. It was 10,000 sq. feet if it was one.

Tom was immediately struck by how beautiful the home was. In fact, when Tina had told him about the Labor Day celebration he had missed the detail about where the event was being held. And due to their schedule differences he had flown down from Northern California separately from Tina. Upon arriving at the house, a well-tanned young man had led him back to "party central" where he currently stood waiting to be greeted.

The way Tina had prepared him for the party, he thought it was going to be held at a country club or, at a minimum, something other than a private residence. Actually the dimensions of the Andersons' home certainly qualified as country club in terms of size and amenities. Its location, inside of a gated community on one of the few peninsulas jutting out into the Pacific Ocean, certainly gave one the feeling of exclusivity. The patio and pool area were beautifully designed and expansive. If the view of the immaculate pool wasn't good enough for you, you just needed to look up to the horizon for a panoramic view of the Pacific.

The terraced landscape was artfully designed to provide every guest with a unique view of either beautiful garden areas or breathtaking views of the rolling coastal hills or the Pacific Coast.

Ken and Amber Anderson had certainly done well. Not that their wealth intimidated Tom, but it did give him pause regarding the manner in which Tina had been raised and the level of expectations she might have going forward, should their relationship progress to a higher level.

"Tom?" he heard from behind him. Turning around he saw the stereotypical 40-something, successful Southern California man. "Ken Anderson," Tina's father announced as he extended his well-tanned and calloused right hand. "Welcome to our home. Sorry about the wait. It's kind of crazy around here with the party today and everything. Can I get you anything? Beer? Wine? Cocktail?"

"Water or a soda would be great, thanks."

"You and Tina are the first to arrive so the staff isn't completely set-up out here yet. Oh, there she is," Ken said referring to an attractive young girl dressed in tan shorts and a white top. "Billie, please get Mr. Daniels a Perrier, thanks." Whether having a waitstaff was a daily occurrence or not, it was clear that Ken Anderson was familiar with the process and expected whatever he asked for to be done immediately.

"Right away," she responded.

"Thanks."

Just at that moment Tom was enveloped from behind by a bear hug from young Tina. After a gentle kiss on the cheek she said, "Well I see you two have already met. Sorry Tom. I got hung up chatting with Mom."

The three of them were then joined by a stunningly beautiful woman. If Tom had not already known that Tina was an only child, he would have sworn that this was her slightly older sister.

"Mom, this is Tom. Tom, my Mom, Amber," she announced proudly.

"So nice to finally meet you Tom," Amber said very graciously. "Tina has told us so much about you."

"Well thank you for having me over. I must say straight off, what a phenomenal home you have here. Simply gorgeous," Tom replied.

Tom thought to himself whether the older version of himself was referring to the home or Amber when he threw out the word "gorgeous".

"Well thank you. I am just so sorry it has taken us so long to get together. But today has actually worked out just right. The rest of the crowd won't be here for another hour or so. That gives us some time to get to know one another," Amber said with a tone suggesting that the timing was by no means an accident. The knowing look between Tina and her mother was one of mutual respect for their logistics prowess.

"Well why don't we all have a seat?" Ken suggested, pointing to one of the many seating areas in the shade. Tina immediately bounced over to the cushioned rattan love-seat, motioning for Tom to join her, while Ken and Amber took the other two seats facing the couple.

"Here you are Mr. Daniels," Billie said as she appeared out of nowhere with Tom's water. "Can I get

anyone else anything?"

"I'll have a Corona. Girls?" Ken asked.

"Well I know it's a little early, but I think this occasion calls for some Champs. Billie please have Stephen open up the champagne," Amber said, receiving an approving smile and nod from Tina.

"Be right back," Billie responded with a smile.

Tom took a long sip from his water and also took a long look at the unlikely gathering that he found himself to be a part of . "Where is this going?" he thought to himself.

Tom's observation from the peanut gallery was that he was watching two guys who had robbed the cradle. Tina was very pretty and the Mom had either incredible genes or had taken a picture of her daughter with her to her plastic surgeon and said, "This!"

After some very small talk about the beautiful weather and home, and a brief conversation that confirmed to Tom that the callouses on Ken's hand were from time spent on the links by a scratch golfer. Billie returned with the beer and champagne. A brief welcome toast from Amber followed, creating a very pleasant, positive vibe at Casa de Anderson.

"So," Ken started. Was an introduction to discussing the direction of the Hi-tech industry on its way? Possibly a solicitation of Tom's opinion about the real estate market, the source of Ken's millions, and its impact on the fluctuating economy? A sporting discussion about the tight pennant race between the two regional California baseball rivals, the Giants and the Dodgers?

No such luck.

"Tina tells us you two are getting pretty tight. Just wondering where this is going?" Ken stated rather directly.

"Daddy!" Tina reacted.

"Kenneth!" Amber admonished.

"What? What did I do?" He asked his family. "I'm sorry Tom, and I assume you prefer that to Tommy?" he asked revealing how Tina must have been gushing about him to her parents. Tom's closed eye nod was enough for Ken.

Tina looked up to the sky as her father continued, "Well Tom here is about all Tina can talk about lately and since we are all here, I thought it would be good to get his take on where this is going. That's all"

"I want to apologize for my husband, Tom," Amber said. "While Tina was very excited about our getting to meet you, the only grilling that is supposed to happen today is when the steaks are on the barbeque." She stated with a finishing glare toward her mildly amused husband.

"I get the sense he doesn't really care one way or the other. He just likes to screw with people," Tom observed.

"That's OK. Frankly, I'm glad you broached the subject," Tom said calmly. "I have to admit I was a little apprehensive coming down here to meet you, particularly given the whole age issue. I'm not sure how I would react to my daughter dating someone that was the same age as I."

There. It was out there.

"Really? I didn't know you were in your 50's?" Ken shared.

"Daddy! My God!" Tina yelled looking toward her mother for help.

"Well I have a few years yet, as I'm guessing the both of you do," Tom said.

"I am starting to like you Mr. Daniels," Amber said reaching out to pat the top of Tom's hand. "It's been a number of years, but I fondly remember my 40's and thank you for your poor eyesight."

"Confirmed…Medical science, not genetics," Tom concluded.

"Really! Well good for you two. You're going to have to share your secrets," Tom said prompting knowing glances amongst the three Andersons.

"Well, to the point, we are enjoying time together. As you know, you raised quite a special woman here," Tom said, immediately feeling the grasp of Tina's hand.

"Tina tells me you have children," Amber mentioned.

"I do. Two. Brad is 15 and Jamie is 12, going on 20," Tom responded.

"Almost as old as you T!" her father chimed in, giggling his way back into the conversation.

"What now?" he asked when his comment resulted in a punch from his wife.

Tom chuckled, thoroughly appreciating Ken's humor and starting to think about how much he would enjoy a round of golf with this guy.

"Well that's great," Amber said trying to recover. "Teenagers. Challenging years," she said looking at Tina. Keeping her gaze on Tina, she asked, "You all getting along ok?"

"We haven't exactly met yet. Tom is very sensitive about introducing a new woman into their lives right now," Tina tried to explain. "But we're working on it."

The real elephant in the room had finally been exposed.

"It's complicated," Tom stated.

"I liked that movie," Ken shared with a growing smile.

"Me too," agreed Tom. "But sometimes living a real life version of it is a little challenging. We're taking things gradually." With that the gentle touch Tina had on Tom's hand turned into more of a grip as she tried to pull him back from getting into too much detail.

The surprised look on Amber's face suggested that the version of Tina and Tom's relationship she had heard from her daughter had a different speed to it. The looks exchanged between the two women indicated that they needed to have a clarifying conversation ...later.

The doorbell in the front of the house broke an awkward silence.

"Well at least we don't have to sit through picking out silver patterns this weekend, do we Thomas?" Ken laughed. "C'mon Tom. Looks like folks are starting to arrive. Let me take you down below and show you my new putting green while the girls greet the guests."

"Well that was a little different show than I expected," Tom shared with Liv.

"How so?"

"The age issue seemed almost nothing compared to the engagement with Brad and Jamie."

"I agree with the word engagement, but with whom is

the question," Liv said. "But, that is something for you to work through later. We have someplace to go before we are finished."

"Really?" Tom asked. "Am I almost finished?"

"Unlike Carin and your mother, I am not one to get too picky about your choice of words, but I would caution your casual use of the word 'finished'. But, yes our time together is coming to an end."

"I can't say I am disappointed. You painted a pretty gloomy picture of what is to be: divorce; at-risk kids; strange relationship behavior; and stranger grooming habits," Tom shared.

"Once again, I want to suggest a correction. Neither I nor my friends had anything to do with the nature of the future you saw painted. Everything that has been shared with you – past, present, and future — was created by your hand.

"While you were certainly provided with a few challenges early in your life, how you have reacted to them then, now, and in the future has been entirely up to you.

"Mr. Daniels, how your life proceeds from here is a indeed a question mark. Nothing is set in stone, so the jury, so to speak, is still out and you still have the opportunity to present your closing argument."

* * *

An awkward silence was interrupted by a loud crack and a brief intense flash of light, as though someone had turned a light switch on and that switch controlled the sun. Tom was no longer at the Anderson estate. He was on the patio deck of a multi-story structure overlooking a scene that was one-third rolling hills, one-third golf course, and one-third vineyard. For a moment he wondered if the flash he thought he experienced was that "LIGHT" referred to by many as the light seen before you die. The beauty he saw certainly qualified as "heavenly".

As he looked around to get his bearings, two things were apparent: 1. He was completely alone. There was no Liv, no Carin, no Love, no family, no kids, no Denise, no Tina, no nobody; and 2. Unless the standard for entering the pearly gates were lower than that which he had always been led to believe, after what he had observed this evening, he probably was not on the A List for entry.

So if he wasn't in heaven, where was he? He slid open the glass door that separated the patio from the main structure to see what appeared to be a very lavish condo. It was perfectly appointed with a pleasing color scheme of natural colors with bold black accents. He could see a living room with very comfortable overstuffed furniture flowing into a media room, an ample kitchen, dining room, bedroom and bath.

He was struck by the exquisite taste of the decor and amazed that the appointments also included an extraordinary array of electronics and audio options. It also appeared that he could activate just about anything in the house from anywhere in the house. Pretty damn cool.

So where was this place and why was he here?

And, where was everybody else?

It finally dawned on him that he was in his Man Cave. Not the home that he had made with Denise and the kids, or the shelter from the rain he'd found on the side of the hill, but the Man Cave he apparently might have had without Denise and the kids.

Quiet.

Orderly.

Sterile.

Empty.

And it was remarkably *empty* considering the material goods that were contained within it.

But where was he really? Obviously his family was not there. The abundance of material things suggested he was successful in this world, at least financially. But he didn't *feel* successful. And he wondered:

"Where was he?"

"Who was he?"

"How did he get here?"

Weren't those the questions that Love had posed?

Love had done a pretty good job of getting his mind off of his car accident and providing a crisp synopsis of his past. She had jogged his memory with her visit and while there were many other events which had influenced him, she had narrowed things down to the biggies that defined *how he got there* and *who he was*.

Tom flashed on the question he had posed to Carin, what seemed to be days ago: "Where is Love?" She had congratulated him on something at that time and he had been confused by her compliment.

Then it hit him. He was asking about what had become of the beautiful spirit Love who had shown him his past and Carin was talking about the concept…the emotion.

Where's Love?

That was indeed the question. While it was just now hitting him, he concluded that it didn't take a rocket scientist to figure out the consistent message from his 3 spiritual visitations. He was focused on work and providing himself and his family with all the creature comforts and opportunities that his income could deliver. While doing so, he had sacrificed time with his family, missing out on the opportunities to share life experiences. It was the same conversation he had had with Dee many times.

Moral of the story: Find a better balance. Done.

Change and spend more time with family. Check.

But something deeper was happening here. As he took in his surroundings, his heart started to pound and his real heart started to ache.

Why was this bothering him so much? He had solved hundreds of tough business and personal challenges in his life and wasn't this just another one? What troubled him most was the fact that the question itself was bothering him. He had received the message loud and clear that his relationship with his family was suffering. He needed to re-prioritize his life. Do so, problem solved. Situation-Solution, done.

The irony of the situation became apparent to him as he realized that just as the opulent condo in which he was standing was missing something, so too would the simple act of re-scheduling his life. It was too simple of a fix. Love was not about his executing his parental and marital duties. Love was not being physically present.

Where's Love?

There was something that he now realized was more important and needed to come first. It was something that if addressed, would solve the rest of his issues.

He had already logically deduced that if he re-prioritized and acted on that re-prioritization, the relationship with his wife and kids would be improved. Everyone would be happy and as in the Age of Aquarius, "Love would steer the stars!"[3] But a fatal flaw in his logic appeared and was rooted in the fact that his family loved him whether he was there or not. The pain that his family was experiencing from his absence was there *because* the loved him. Not the other way around.

One of the Dad-isms, the phrases that he was so fond of and that his kids had referenced in his earlier visit with Carin, came from his work experience and he had also applied it to his personal life: *it's more important to understand the questions than to know the answers.*

Tom had arrived at this wisdom by observing and experiencing many scenarios in which well meaning, very competent business people had made huge mistakes by zealously executing solutions to the wrong problems. "Putting the cart before the horse" still applied to many in business, as they put their ownership, and potential recognition, for a solution above a thoughtful deliberation of the issues at hand.

Tom had the benefit of having observed some of the best in Silicon Valley. Among other qualities, they all shared one: the ability to distill numerous data points into a manageable few and arrive first at the key questions to answer/problems to solve. Then and only then, did they select the proper path to follow.

---

3. "Aquarius/Let the Sunshine In"©1967 from the musical Hair by James Rado & Gerome Ragni (lyrics), and Galt MacDermot (music).

He suddenly felt embarrassed, stupid, and relieved, all at the same time. He could finally answer Carin's question. Everything that the lessons of his 30 year childhood had taught him had also provided him the answer to the question and explained why it was so important.

From his idyllic childhood, through his obsessive desire to compete, and his reliance on the memory of his late brother for guidance and motivation, to his success in overcoming, at least so far, his reliance on alcohol, there was one common thread: His Love.

It wasn't about love coming *to* him. It was about love coming *from* him. Everything he had and was came from his love for: achievement, people, and most importantly, himself.

He had overcome many challenges that required a level of pain and suffering. But the challenge before him now was not one requiring hard work. It was simple: Let his love flow and the tactical parts would resolve themselves.

He briefly recalled the line from the old Clapton song, Let it Rain: "Until I found the way to love, it's harder said than done."[4]

A warmth and calmness enveloped him. A relief and fatigue also hit him as he walked out to the deck and laid down on the chaise lounge.

So comfortable.

So drained.

He dozed off.

---

4. (B. Bramlett & E. Clapton, 1970)

CHAPTER V
T H E   N E W   N O R M

Tom was jiggled awake by what he sensed was an earthquake.

Being a native Californian, he instinctively estimated that it was only a "2 point 5er" on the Richter Scale. He could tell by the light, or lack of it, and the temperature, that he was back on the hill. Reality flooded back to him, distancing him from the comfort of the New Man Cave that he had started to buy into as being real. But he was back where he started. He had not gone anywhere. He was where he had holed up after the accident: on the slope, up a creek with no paddle, in his more natural Man

Cave.

He was exhausted. But he thought that what he had just experienced was probably the only thing in this or any other world that made his current predicament on the slope desirable. He had clearly lost his mind and considered if this was how it was all going to end. Tom had never been a religious man, but considered himself to be spiritual. He flashed on his childhood and the way he once understood the difference between the Catholic and Jewish religions. With his good friends being nearly evenly split between Catholics and Jews, he just thought the only differences were the days that they couldn't play due to church/temple activities, and that you had to finagle an invitation for dinner at their houses on different days to cash in on the their great holiday menus. If only life's choices were that simple.

He also recalled the conversation with his therapist, Dr. Santiago, all those years ago at the beginning of his treatment for alcoholism. After the results of some of the psychological tests came back they had discussed religion briefly.

"So Tom, did you go to church a lot as a kid?" Doc asked.

"No, not really. With the exception of weddings and a couple of funerals, I can only remember going to church a couple of times with friends."

"Interesting. No religious training?"

"Not growing up, but I studied a little about eastern religion and philosophy at school, why do you ask?"

"Because your spirituality quotient is off the charts. Don't take my questions the wrong way. That spirituality is going to be very helpful as we work together."

Would his spirituality help him now? And if so, how? Was this how it ended?

Tom hoped not. He thought about Denise and the kids. He missed them and the sadness of that was matched by his frustration at not having made better use of his time, his short time on earth. He also regretted not having gotten to know them better and enjoyed their lives together more.

He thought about the events of what seemed to be the last few hours but could have been a matter of minutes. So many questions and so few answers. Or was that the way it was? He had a complicated life between his work, the family, and his social and philanthropic obligations. It all seemed overwhelming to him before his accident.

But there had been no complexity in what Love helped him recall in his past. He knew in his heart and mind how he had become who and what he was.

There was no complexity to the current state of affairs, thank you Carin. The important affairs of the family and marriage were all too clear. While he had wondered what was "slightly off" with his marriage, now he knew. Now he knew.

But more importantly, there were three additional take-aways from Carin's visit. First, it was clear that what was wrong extended beyond just his marital and family relationships. It extended to his relationships with his friends, as well. He also wondered to what extent it also extended into his work life. While Carin had not taken him there, would the needed adjustments also make a positive impact on his work?

The second was that "slightly" was a gross underestimation of the fundamental dysfunction in his life. The life that he had created for himself.

And that was the third biggie: everything that Carin had showed him was of his own making, just as Liv had said. While Tom was saddened by the current state of affairs presented by his Three Ladies of the Night, this last realization gave him a sense of hope and empowerment. If it was of his doing, it could very well be solved by his actions.

The version of his future to which Liv had exposed him was filled with awkwardness and heartache that exceeded any challenges or injuries his current situation on the side of the hill presented, just as she had promised. Liv hadn't said much, but the glimpse she provided into his future had spoken volumes, with an abundance of clarity.

From the potential dissolution of his relationship and marriage with Denise to the entry into what he kept thinking of as a "perverse" relationship with a younger woman; to the negative impact on his children; and the vacuous world represented by his well-appointed Man Cave, his current course and speed were obviously leading him to a place that he did not want to be.

But these were only possibilities, not eventualities.

As Tom thought through all that had occurred during his rather active evening, he was taking stock of who he was and what he was capable of, what was important and what would happen from here. He thought of applying his approach to business problems to create a plan to "correct" his world and avoid the Liv world. Then he laughed, remembering that it was precisely his work life that was causing much of his woe; perhaps it wasn't the best place to look for solutions!

When faced with tough situations at work he would draw on various business skills in acquiring relevant data, distilling the issues, and determining the proper course of action. It was his experience in doing this which made him effective and successful. He had often referred to his experience and wisdom as his "grey hair". His laughter came from his realization that what Love had led him to re-live, was his life's "grey hair".

He wasn't sure if it was his spirituality or a simple hope he had always had that there was some master plan or grand scheme of a Higher Power for him that would result in his happiness. But it was now clear to him that everything he had experienced in his rather "dull" life had prepared him to deal with his current situation. The ups and downs; the joys and tragedies; the victories and failures had all added up to his ability to face and fix his current issues.

Now if someone could just find him and he could get to work — work on the job that mattered, that is.

* * *

Tom felt another jolt. An aftershock to the first earthquake?

"Excuse me Mr. Daniels? We're preparing to land and I need you to bring your seat back up and buckle your seat belt."

"Huh?" A startled Tom Daniels responded.

"We're landing. Please bring your seat up and buckle your seat belt," Dori, the cute, young flight attendant repeated patiently.

"Sure," he said before the words and his consciousness aligned and he was aware of where he was.

Tom looked around the First Class Cabin of the American Airlines 737 to see everyone engaged in their prep activity for the arrival of the flight. He instinctively lifted his leg and stretched it out into the aisle of the plane. Stiff-yes…pain-no. A quick rotation of his neck confirmed he was no longer suffering from a concussion. And it was pretty evident that he was no longer on the side of the hill, huddled in his Man Cave. He was on a friggin' plane. He was heading home.

He was safe, if not sound.

He was going to see his family.

"Man, what the hell was that?!" he thought, half expecting some witty retort from Carin. He started thinking of his time spent watching fantasy-based movies in which the hero awakens with relief, realizing it was all a dream, or had it somehow been implanted in his head. Had he been that influenced by The Wizard of Oz, It's a Wonderful Life, and all the rest?

As the plane landed and taxied to the gate, all of the passengers started their routine activities: quick check of their personal appearance; collection of their personal belongings; and checking the incredibly important voice-mail messages that had accumulated during the 4 hour flight from Chicago to San Jose. And yes, there was the idiot who just had to stand up before the seat belt sign went off, flying into another passenger when the plane finally came to a halting stop at the gate.

As Tom unconsciously pulled his iPhone from his bag, he started to find the auto-dial key for his voice-mail when he caught himself. "I wonder if she's picking me up at the curb or at baggage claim?" he thought. The "She" was his wife, Denise. It was kind of a strange thought actually as it really didn't matter. If she was there at baggage claim, she was there. If she wasn't, she wasn't and he would walk to the curb after collecting his checked luggage and wait to be picked-up, just like always.

But this time it seemed to matter and he was hoping she was there. He missed her and for the first time in a long time he was very anxious to see her. He also considered the propriety of buying one of those incredibly practical and convenient belt clips for his cell phone.

He proceeded to text her, "At gate, where r u?"

Almost immediately he received his response, "at bag claim. Welcome home"

"Cool. C u in a few. L U!" he responded as his heart quickened. What was going on? He hadn't used their secret code for "I love you" in a long while but it just came out instinctively.

The normal gate arrival process for the flight attendants, signaled by the pilot's announcement, "Flight attendants, please prepare the cabin for arrival and cross-check," seemed to be progressing at a 'glacial pace'. He laughed out loud as he recalled when he had first heard that phrase: watching (and thoroughly enjoying) the movie The Devil Wears Prada, with Denise.

He was happy to be home and very impatient. He wanted to see Denise and these people were keeping him from getting what he wanted.

It wasn't that he didn't always enjoy returning from his constant business trips, but something was different this time. It really didn't matter what it was, he just missed his wife and wanted desperately to see her.

And then it hit him....his dream or whatever it was...is that why I am feeling different? The question in his mind was followed by the anticipation of another snide comment from Carin, "No shit Sherlock!"

He was fully awake now and marveled at how vivid his dream had been. What also struck him was that he seemed to be able to recall every detail of what had transpired, as though it had really happened. What was even more remarkable, he thought, was that he could count on one hand the number of times he could recall any dream he'd ever had. "Oh well, I must have been really tired," he decided.

Or did the vividness mean it wasn't a dream? He hated those TV shows and movies that explained away all manner of inexplicable happenings with a "dream." But now that he'd been "in the belly of the beast," he was willing to say, "Ok. Whatever. Cool."

However it had occurred, it was now part of his reality.

★ ★ ★

Finally the cattle were being released from the pen. He was moving through the gate area as a remarkably beautiful woman passed him on the way to baggage claim. He looked at her longer than normal, making it a borderline gawk. And then it hit him. She was the identical twin to Love. To his embarrassment and shock, the length of his gaze enabled "Love" to meet his look, as she offered a demure smile, followed by a slightly slutty wink of an eye. And like that, she moved on.

Tom was in shock and stopped in his tracks. As he gathered his wits about him and adjusted the placement of the strap of his laptop bag on his shoulder, he felt a strong bump from behind. He had apparently become one of those distracted people in an airport that don't realize that when the traffic flow is going one way, you can't just stop.

"Excuse you!" an unmistakable voice complained. "Watch it, Bud!" As Tom was about to stop her, he thought better of it. "Carin" hustled by him, turning to deliver a parting shot, "Gawd, some people can be so clueless!" delivered with what Tom could swear was a wry smile of recognition.

"This is pretty damn strange," Tom thought, as he merged back into the long straight corridor that would lead him to his lovely Dee. How long had it been since he called her by her pet name? Too long.

He could see the set of doors that separated the secure terminal area and baggage claim. The doors were positioned just to the right of the exit from the security checkpoint, creating an interesting passing of those about to catch their departing flight and those arriving home. His attention was drawn to a woman walking very fast, apparently just having passed through the security line. She appeared to be very focused and on a very important phone call.

"Holy shit! It's Liv!" he said aloud. He moved slightly to his left to make a soft attempt to intercept her, only to get a reaction that would be best described as disgust. She reacted with an avoiding side-step and briskly moved on.

"No way. Long trip," he mumbled to himself dismissively.

His pace quickened as he approached the doors and burst through them. His wife, his Dee, was waiting for him just to the side of the luggage turnstile. She smiled in an obligatory way. As he reached her, he dropped his computer bag and proceeded to give her a big bear hug that she semi-returned. The length and strength of the contact gave her the opportunity to recover from the initial shock and participate in the activity.

"Did he start drinking again on that flight?" she thought to herself

Dee thought that the aberrant behavior was about to come to an end just as Tommy Boy drew his head back from the smothering embrace and proved her wrong by planting a big, long, wet kiss on her lips.

"Watch my bag, while I go get my luggage," Tom said as he rushed over to the turnstile to retrieve his checked bag. Dee was just starting to get her breath back as Tom returned with the enthusiasm of little boy.

"What are the kids up to?" Tom asked with a sense of purpose.

"They're over at friends' houses," Denise answered, somewhat taken aback by the question.

"Cool, cuz we gotta talk!" he said.

"Well that sounds ominous," Dee said, still flustered and confused by his unusual behavior.

"Really? Well it shouldn't or it won't or I'm not sure what it is."

They headed off to the airport parking garage covering the standard catch-up topics from the previous week while he was out of town. As they approached the car, Tom asked Dee if she minded driving as he was pretty tired from his trip and the flight. His motivation was not only his fatigue but that Dee had driven the family's SUV to the airport and Tom was not particularly fond of driving it. In fact, for some reason, he had no interest in driving any car.

Tom deposited his luggage in the back of the vehicle.

Denise drove the car through the garage to the exit and took care of the parking fees. She then navigated them through the maze of roads towards the freeway.

"So how was the trip? It must have been good judging from your greeting at baggage claim," Dee asked as she merged onto the crowded freeway.

"It was OK. Pretty routine stuff. We're getting ready to launch a new product set into the Enterprise market and just needed to make sure we had everyone's attention and buy-in," Tom answered.

"Flight OK? Did you get upgraded to First?"

"Yes. Thank God. I actually decided not to work on the flight and get some rest," Tom added, still not entirely sure what had or hadn't occurred on the flight and how much rest he had really gotten.

"I also got a chance to do a little thinking," Tom said.

"Really?! How rare!" Dee jabbed.

"Cute. But seriously, I think I need to scale down a little on the work front."

"You mean retire? I didn't think we were in a position to do that yet," Dee responded quickly.

"No no...I wish. You're right, we aren't there yet. But I mean just ratchet it down a couple of notches."

"Oh? What do you mean? I don't want to raise the B.S. flag right away, but we have had this conversation before and before and before."

"And don't forget about that other time," Tom joked, prompting Dee to look over at him and see the wide grin on his face. "You're right. Lots of talk and no action. I know. But it is time to make some changes and with some adjustments at work. I think the stars are now aligning in a way that I can."

Tom's statement hit Denise in a way that made her realize that maybe this time he was singing a different tune. Not only was he the one that was broaching the subject, but for the first time in all of the conversations they had had on the topic, he actually brought up the topic of *how* to accomplish the goal.

Denise had observed Tom's professional skills at work through his and others' descriptions of his activities. She had also interacted with many of his colleagues at various functions and she knew that one of his strengths was his ability to operationalize ideas and strategies. In fact, she had even heard him referred to as an "operational machine" on one occasion. The mere fact that he had mentioned that he had thought of a way in which he could change his work/life balance, indicated to her that maybe this was something substantive, not just "make Dee feel good" talk.

"Wow! That's great. But I hope you'll excuse my

skepticism. What's up?" she asked, reminding him again in a not-so-subtle way that she had heard similar words before.

"The details are pretty involved, but suffice to say that I should be able to make work more predictable. But more importantly, I want to make work more controllable.

"My cardiologist told me one time that he never had a patient suffering from heart failure tell him that he wished he had spent more time in the office. And no, there is nothing wrong with my heart, but that comment and some other thoughts got me to thinking about how I might be letting my life, the part that matters, pass me by."

Denise was so shocked by this revelation that she almost missed the exit to the freeway that would lead them over the bridge to their home. Her abrupt double lane change prompted Tom to ask, "You OK?"

"Yeah, I'm fine. More importantly, are you?" she asked.

"Good one. And fair. I've always told you that the concept of the wife being the 'better half' in a marriage applied to us more than other couples. It's just taken me a little longer to arrive at the conclusion you've been talking about for the last few years."

"Well don't let my sarcasm derail you, Baby. You're on a role. Keep going," Dee encouraged.

"I'm not saying that work is going away, but enough is enough. I owe you and the kids more of me. And I owe me, more of you."

Denise was glad that it was dark outside and in the car, as she felt that if Tom saw the tears starting to well up in her eyes it might stop him from continuing with his train of thought.

"Anyway, it's time for change and change it will be," Tom proclaimed.

After a few minutes of commute hypnosis, Tom broke the silence. "I have something else I want to ask you," signaling what Denise hoped would not be a segue to a less positive subject. She like this one.

"How are you?" he asked

"What do you mean?" she asked, taken aback by the off-the-wall question.

"I mean, how are you? How are you feeling about you and you and me?" Tom clarified.

"Well I guess we're finished with all the fun talk. Don't get me wrong, I appreciate the question, but I hope you can appreciate that you are kind of surprising me here... no shocking me is more accurate. To answer your question, I'm good. And I'm starting to think that I'm on my way to being better."

"I know I'm hitting you with a lot and we can talk later about details. I'm just worried that I haven't been the husband and friend I should have been. And because of that, you may not have been able to do all the things you wanted to do."

"What do you mean? I'm OK and keeping very busy," she replied, turning off the freeway toward their neighborhood.

"This probably isn't a good time to get into it, but it just seems that with the kids getting older, maybe you would want to get more involved in charity activities or other non-kid things. And if I can be true to my commitment to you, I can help cover some of the kids' stuff."

"I really don't know what to say, Tom," a stunned Dee admitted.

"It's not like you have to or even want to, I just know how much you are capable of giving and want you to know that I am supportive of whatever you want to do.

"Not that we can't keep chatting when we get home, but here's my last brain dump before we arrive: with summer coming up, how about you taking some golf lessons and joining me in playing with some of the couples at the Club? We could even sneak out some evenings and play some twilight golf together."

"Well I knew this conversation was too good to be true," Dee laughed. "I have to tell you that you have made me very happy with everything you've been thinking about. But I have a confession to make. As much as I enjoy your passion for golf and following your exploits with the Boys, golf bores the shit out of me! Please tell me that golf is not a condition for us to do everything else you talked about, Mr. Daniels!"

With that, Tom started laughing. It wasn't just a giggle. It was a deep, uncontrollable, hurting-stomach-muscles,, pee-in-your-pants laugh that he had not enjoyed for a long time.

As Dee joined in the laughter she said, "Oh my. This has been quite a surprise—a very pleasant surprise. I must say as much as you're talking about scaling back your work, I may start being more of a fan of your trips to Chicago."

Dee turned the car onto their street. Tom's physical condition provided indisputable evidence he had not sustained any injuries from his "accident" and his car being safely parked in the driveway, resolved any lingering doubt as to whether the accident had occurred at all. Despite this evidence the view of their home at the end of the court gave him a feeling that he had indeed been rescued.

He was home and damn happy about it.

"Well I just gotta say, I'm thrilled to be home and have you as my wife. Will you still have me, Mrs. Daniels?" Tom proposed in an adolescent way.

"Well," she chuckled, failing to control her amusement. "Yes, I guess so – for better or worse I think is what I committed to."

"For better, Dee, I promise. From here on out, for better."

CHAPTER VI
HIS WORLD

To be comforted by your touch,
To be proud to share your name,
To be humbled by my good fortune,
To be amazed by your inner beauty,
To be aroused by the sight of you,
To be envied by all who know you,
To learn from your unique view of the world,
To be grateful for how you've made me better,
To be thankful for every day we've had,
To be excited by the promise of every day to come,
And to be safe in your arms,
Is to live in the warmth of your Love.

CHAPTER VII
MY BREADCRUMBS

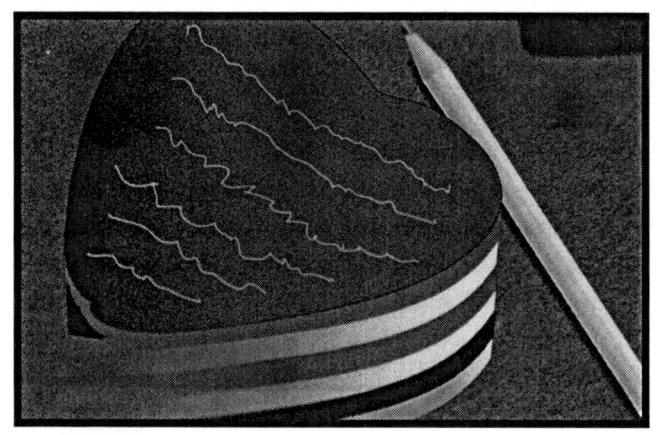

While *In Pursuit of Love* is a work of fiction, much of the story is based on my rather unremarkable life. I related many anecdotes from my youth and adult past, changing names and certain details to protect the innocent...actions that did not materially affect the credibility of the story.

With full confidence in your ability to distill the relevant aspects of Tom's past, I encourage your examination into the issues of addiction, life's balancing act, social competition, and young athlete's health and humbly offer you a few random yet purposeful notes.

- "Hi, I'm Jim, and I'm an alcoholic."
  Addiction is serious business for the addict, the friends and families of the addict, and society in general. *In Pursuit of Love* is not intended to be a guide to recovery or a directive for those of you who are suffering. The portion of the story that touches this subject is intended to share a story of someone lucky enough to have made some smart decisions and had the support along the way that resulted in his finding a happier, more productive and fulfilling life.

  There is no shame or guilt in asking for help...just hope.

- How green is your grass?
  There may be great value to emulating others' ideas of comfort, recreation, and product utility, but when the motive moves from utility and actual personal values to a "me too" motive or cause, or a "me first" motive, then we are getting into the ugly of it all and you may start to become the Joneses.

  This may come off as being against the accumulation of the finer things in life... not at all. Good for you if you can afford it, just be prepared for the garage sale.[5]

- At the Heart of Youth Sports
  Young Tom's premature end to his athletic career was lifted straight out of young Jim's life. While my personal experience was impacted in no small way by what we now consider the archaic medical knowledge

---

5. Reference to the late genius George Carlin and his phenomenal and poignant comedy routine about "Stuff"

and diagnostic tools of many years ago, the need for young athletes and their parents to be attentive to health of young athletes knows no era.

That heart flutter, that persistent pain, that dizziness, that "anything" needs to be watched for, recognized, and examined. It may be nothing, but medical professionals are the best ones to help us determine if it is a something. The "team" (aka adults) needs to be supportive and attentive to the process and appropriately responsive to issues that may arise.

Winning isn't everything, living is.

- Your Personal Teeter Totter

  In our compressed, complicated, and compartmentalized lives, most of us grapple with this. In addition to what insight and inspiration this story may have provided, I suggest you take a look at Jeff Patnaude's book, Living Simultaneously. In it, Jeff states, "Most of us have operated in such overload for so long that the norm becomes The Way of Too- too much, too fast, too often, and perhaps too little, too late. The universe offers each of us an invitation to the bountiful feast of a life of playfulness, laughter, love and creativity. Whether or not we attend the party is a matter of personal choice. Discovering balance within the flow of our lives is the goal."[6]

  For some of us living by this sage advice may be very challenging to do, but every journey starts with a first step. I suggest that you ask yourself the question, "Is it time to start *my* journey?"

---

6. Used by permission from Jeffery Patnaude from his book "Living Simultaneously" ©2001 Jeffery Patnaude, Rhino Press.

ACKNOWLEDGMENTS

- To Dr. Santiago Estrada, for without your timely and life-saving guidance I would not be here.
- To Charles Dickens, for your Time Machine.
- To George French, a life coach before his time, for the Life Lessons Learned so early.
- To my Family, for your patience through my 30 year adolescence.
- To my Children, thank you for being my heroes and mentors.
- To Bob Kanegis, storyteller extraordinaire, for asking me "Why?"
- To my Bruin Family, for your support when you had no obligation to provide it.
- To Jeff Patnaude, for the guidance and the joy of a Simultaneous Life.
- To my Brothers…what I wouldn't give to have just one more game of Ball-up.
- To Everyone who is managing through the challenges of addiction…Yes, you can!
- To Everyone who is not managing through the challenges of addiction….Yes, you can!
- To my wife, Dora, while we know It's All About You, thanks for making me feel that is all about me.

RECOMMEND THIS BOOK
IN PURSUIT OF LOVE

OR VISIT US ONLINE
www.facebook.com/ItsAllAboutHer.org

MORE BOOKS BY LIBRARY TALES PUBLISHING
www.librarytalespublishing.com
www.facebook.com/librarytalespublishing
www.twitter.com/librarytales